THE WATER'S EDGE

THE WATER'S EDGE

Karin Fossum

WINDSOR
PARAGON

First published 2009
by Havill Secker
This Large Print edition published 2010
by BBC Audiobooks Ltd
by arrangement with
The Random House Group Ltd

Hardcover ISBN: 978 1 408 46098 6
Softcover   ISBN: 978 1 408 46099 3

British Library Cataloguing in Publication Data available

Printed and bound in Great Britain by
CPI Antony Rowe, Chippenham and Eastbourne

A long, gentle hill sloped down from the main road to the loch known as Loch Bonna. At the edge of the water was a beach with sharp stones and a steep drop further out. A narrow tarmac road wound its way like a grey ribbon between the fields, the houses lay arranged in colourful rows, their verandas and balconies facing north towards the water. In the distance well-kept farms with grey and white farmhouses and red barns could be seen. There was Fagre Vest which belonged to Waldemar Skagen whose horse, Evidence, was grazing inside an enclosure. East of the lake lay Fagre Øst, owned by Skagen's brother-in-law. A rainbow formed a colourful arch between the two farms, a shower of rain had crossed the sky recently and the sun was breaking through.

At the top of the road overlooking Loch Bonna was a shop, which had lately become a branch of the Kiwi supermarket chain; a bright spark in marketing had decided to dress the employees in green uniforms. On the front door was a notice ordering schoolchildren to leave their rucksacks outside, they shoplifted constantly, nicking cigarettes and sweets.

Signe Lund was sitting by the till, groceries gliding past her on the belt, daydreaming as teenagers do. She could see Loch Bonna through the window and Fagre Vest with its undulating pink and yellow fields. On a field below Svart Ridge was a small mound with pretty rowan trees, it rose like an island in a sea of wheat. The mound with its trees and bushes held a secret, a small earth cellar known to only a few. She was thinking of it now. The bittersweet memory lingered still.

1

CHAPTER 1

No one saw him walk through the woods; no one saw what he was carrying. A modest burden for a grown man, yet it caused him difficulty, his steps were faltering and he stumbled. From time to time he would stop, gasp for air and make noises which sounded like whimpering. Then he would stagger on as quickly as he could. He walked underneath the trees like an old man, weighed down by it all, weighed down by horror and tears. It was so overwhelming that his knees threatened to buckle; he kept looking over his shoulder, his head twitching nervously. He increased his speed as he approached a cluster of trees. He did not wish to discard his burden casually on the ground; he wanted this precise cluster of trees, which would serve as a kind of monument. This last scrap of decency comforted him, he was still a human being, he had feelings, many of them good ones. Again he looked over his shoulder: there was not a soul around. He remained standing, sensing every sound as his heart pounded. The forest was like a huge organism, it breathed, it watched him, it condemned him with its deep, ominous rustling. How could you stoop so low? the forest intoned, no human being will ever smile at you with warmth or love, not after this.

He had reached the cluster of trees.

He squatted down.

He placed his burden on a bed of soft moss. He got up and wiped the sweat from his brow; it felt hot. This does not look good, he thought, not in

3

any way. Emotions surged inside him, a mixture of panic and rage, nothing ever worked out for him, it was a mistake, the whole thing. How could it have happened? Horrified, he buried his face in his hands, they smelled like hot iron. He tasted fear in his mouth and felt it in his blood and in his lungs. Fate had played a mean trick on him and dealt him a rotten hand; now he was being hurled down towards condemnation and denunciation. Hanging's too good for him, people would say, lock him up and throw away the key; a man like him should never be allowed out again. He lurched a little to the side, he felt weak at the knees. I have to go now, he thought, I need to get out of here, I must get back to my car, drive home to my house, lock the door and draw the curtains. Huddle in a corner and listen out in case anyone should come. But I won't answer the door, he decided, I'll lock myself in, I won't be able to cope with this! He raised a clenched fist towards the sky, towards God, who had created him with such strong urges, but who would not allow him to satisfy them the way he wanted to.

His car was parked close to a road barrier a little way off. He walked briskly without looking back and moved as quickly as he could through the forest. It was not long before he saw the barrier and his car. And something else: something was moving, something red and white against the green. He stopped abruptly. A man and a woman were out walking. His first thought was to hide between the spruces, but at the last second he thought better of it and continued, averting his eyes, along the short distance he had left. The storm raged inside him with renewed force. This is fatal, he thought, this will be my undoing, those two people walking towards me, they will remember me and tell the whole world. We saw him and we can describe him clearly, they would say, he was wearing a blue anorak. And the hunt would begin. He did not look up until he reached his car and he met the woman's eyes for a fleeting moment. It surprised him that she smiled at him, a broad and friendly smile. When he failed to return her smile and stared at her in horror, she looked puzzled. The couple continued past the barrier and into the forest. The woman, however, turned one last time and looked after him.

CHAPTER 2

They were a couple, but they had been married for many years and they no longer held hands. The woman was wearing a raspberry red coat, the man a white windbreaker. He was constantly one step ahead of her, tall, self-assured and fit. The woman watched him furtively while she contemplated her own thoughts. Her husband was a man who owned his space; now he owned this forest and he helped himself to it. The vegetation was compressed beneath his feet as he walked, dry twigs snapped and the woman struggled to keep up with him. They were out of step. They had thoughts they didn't want to share or admit. But they had gone out for a walk together, it was their habit and they needed habits, habits held them together and made the world predictable.

It was a surprisingly warm September day. The

man unbuttoned his jacket and a gust of wind made it flap like a sail. He rummaged around in his pockets, looking for a cigarette.

'Reinhardt,' the woman said. 'It's ever so dry around here.'

Her voice was devoid of authority, it was more like a pitiful plea. He snarled in irritation; he was not one of those men who allowed themselves to be reprimanded. He closed his lips around the filter of the cigarette and lit it with a Zippo lighter. His irises were blue like the ocean with golden flecks, his nose was sharp and looked good in profile.

The woman chose to say nothing; experience had taught her this was her best option. She focused on the forest floor, there were tufts of grass and the odd dip; every now and again roots would crisscross the path. She glanced quickly at her husband: he was much taller than her, broader, stronger, he always led the way. She had suppressed her own views for years because he was so argumentative and opinionated. Now she worried about the dry ground and the burning cigarette.

The light that once existed between us has been extinguished, she thought sadly, nothing shines any more, we should have had a child. A child would have brought us closer, it would have united us and made us good people. This is what she believed. But the years had passed and no child had come; her husband had said no and she hadn't dared cross him. Whenever she raised the subject, he became sullen and would jut out his chin while she lowered her eyes and grew silent. We're all right as we are, aren't we, he would say, we both work full-time, there's the house and the garden, we're mortgaged to the hilt. How do people find the time, he pushed on, how do they find the money? She offered him no reply, but she noticed that people did find the time. She also noticed that they looked exhausted, torn between the demands of their children, their careers and their personal needs. But the moment their child crawled up on their lap, they became radiant, and she longed with all of her heart for this glow. That unique glow she had seen in her friends' eyes.

Her husband had finished smoking, the tobacco still glowed red. Suddenly he flicked the stub away, it leapt into the air and sparks flew in an arc. The woman followed it with her eyes: it landed in the heather, still smoking.

'Reinhardt,' she begged. 'Stamp it out!'

Reinhardt took a few steps to the side and ground the butt with exaggerated force using the sole of his shoe.

'You worry too much, Kristine.'

She shrugged defensively, she dared not show any greater rebellion than that. The sun, which would soon set, let its last rays spill out between the trees. And Kristine, too, unbuttoned her jacket. She brushed her long hair away from her cheeks and her forehead. It was thick and brown with auburn streaks. She was petite, her face was small with a high domed forehead and round cheeks. She had tiny hands and feet, and indeed her husband would in more affectionate moments call her his 'doll'. Reinhardt, too, ran his fingers through his hair. A short, sandy-coloured tuft stuck up at the front, it looked like a shark's fin. They were heading towards Lake Linde; this was their usual destination, every Sunday after lunch. Kristine was struck by their routine life, the habits that trapped them, the old grooves which held them in place. No one ever broke the rhythm. They left their house together every morning and said goodbye outside the Central Hospital, where she worked as a receptionist. Reinhardt drove on to the offices of Hafslund where he worked with security systems. They ate dinner together and watched television, side by side in front of the blue glare. Afterwards Reinhardt would sit in front of his computer and play games while Kristine did the housework. It really bothered her that he spent so much time on the computer, she did not think a grown man of thirty-six should be playing at wizards and dragons. Not only did his eyes shine with excitement but he often indulged in childish outbursts, which embarrassed her. He would curse and swear appallingly or he would shout out in triumph when he managed to slay an enemy. In addition he talked incessantly, he had an opinion about everything and he had a solution to every problem. They never talked about themselves or how they felt. Most of it had already been said and, in her darker moments, Kristine felt that they had become strangers. At night she would lie awake for long periods breathing against the wall, while Reinhardt snored violently. At times he would take her with an intensity that came close to scaring her. This is my life, she thought, I won't get any more than this. I could leave him, but where would I go, what would I say? He is reliable and faithful, he never hits me and every month he receives a pay cheque which is considerably bigger than mine. She was weighed down by these thoughts as they

8

walked through the forest. Are other people happy, she wondered, is there something wrong with us, is there something that we've failed to grasp?

Reinhardt was way ahead of her. Out of the corner of her eye, she could see his moving shadow. She felt permanently guilty. No matter how hard she looked, she could discover no positive feelings towards him and she felt like a traitor. Her betrayal brought her to her knees. She did not dare confront him, cause him to doubt her or make demands, because then he might expose her: you don't love me, did you honestly think I didn't know? Do you really think I don't know that you're faking? She plodded after him on the path, her thoughts making her cheeks burn. They were aiming for Lake Linde where they would stand on the shore for a few minutes as usual; the water always made her feel better. The water would extinguish the fire in her cheeks and cool her down. She would ponder the ruins of the old settlement by the shore, small, modest circles of stone. Once they had contained families with children, living and working, falling ill and dying, brief moments of happiness and despair. It was hard to imagine how people used to manage with so little. Between them, Reinhardt and she had two hundred and fifty square metres they hardly ever used, they sat next to each other on the sofa in front of the television while the bedrooms waited for children who never came, for friends who never stayed over.

Only the tallest trees were touched by the sun now. This, Kristine thought, is the best time of year. Not the hysteria of summer, or the storms of

9

autumn, or the cold of winter, or even the treacherous late frost or the early spring with its sudden sleet and unpredictable gusts of wind, but September with its unique serenity. Dark cool nights, refreshing mornings. Suddenly she felt exhausted, she was weighed down by so many thoughts and though it was warm, she wrapped her coat around her body more tightly.

'It's Sunday,' Reinhardt said, 'it's Sunday and the weather is fine. And there's not a soul to be seen. Can you believe it?'

She looked up at him with wide green eyes.

'We're here,' she said softly.

He jutted out his chin as he always did when someone corrected him and she loathed that tiny gesture, hated that he could never just nod in agreement. And she despised herself because she was afraid of him. She was constantly on the defensive, she was always on her guard, because he had this hold over her, as if something existed deep inside him that she did not dare face. An image from a childhood fairy tale of a monster slumbering at the bottom of a swamp surfaced in her mind.

'Yes, but all the same,' he countered, 'look how deserted it is. There's not a single tent or a boat here. Lake Linde is a pearl, but people can't be bothered to come up here because they can't drive the whole way.'

'But that's why we like walking here,' she said: 'because it's so peaceful.'

Reinhardt felt in his pockets for another cigarette, the low sun touched his broad cheekbones and his forceful chin. And she recalled the first time she saw him and how he had seemed carved out of granite. There were many edges and protrusions in his broad face, but his eyes were deep-set. On Sundays he skipped shaving and a pale shadow was spreading across his jaw.

'Schoolchildren go camping here,' Kristine remembered. 'If they choose Outdoor Studies. They go canoeing and fishing and they have to get up at three in the morning to hear the wood grouse.'

Reinhardt shrugged. 'I've never really understood the attraction of camping,' he snorted. 'You can rent a cottage up here. With a proper bed and a toilet. When I was a boy,' he went on, 'my dad took me camping. He had an old-fashioned green tent that slept four people, I couldn't bear the smell inside it, and my sleeping bag was ancient and musty. It stank of smoke and earth and paraffin, it smelled of waterproofing chemicals. I couldn't sleep. I couldn't breathe.'

Kristine went over to one of the mounds of grass and stepped inside a stone circle.

'This is where their kitchen must have been,' she called out.

Reinhardt came over to her.

'I wouldn't call that a kitchen,' he smiled. 'More like a fireplace, I'd say.'

She nodded. 'Just think,' she said, 'they would catch fish in the lake and snare birds and hares. What a quiet life it must have been, here by the water.'

Reinhardt entered the circle. He stood towering over her, he was one metre ninety tall and very broad-shouldered.

'In the evenings they would sit by the fire and talk amongst themselves,' she said, 'and when the

11

fire died down they would curl up on the ground under their furs.'

Reinhardt grinned broadly. 'Whereas I turn on my Bang & Olufsen music centre and stretch out in my recliner,' he said. 'Thank God, I'm alive now.'

Kristine went quiet once again. He refused to join in her thinking, he didn't want to ponder life or humanity. He was an enterprising man, rational and self-assured, whereas she felt dizzy when she imagined herself living in another age, where people had different values, where their fears had been different from the ones she lived with. Perhaps they had feared a roaming wolf stalking the half-naked children playing on the shore of Lake Linde.

CHAPTER 3

'We'll go back a different route,' he called out.

He cut through the forest, holding back the branches so they would not swipe her face. Again they walked themselves warm in the low sunshine and after half an hour they stopped for a rest. In front of them lay a clearing surrounded by spruces, an open, golden area with tufts and heather. Then the brutal scene hit them.

'No!' Reinhardt yelled.

And again, a few seconds later. 'No!'

Kristine gave him an uncomprehending look. He was squeezing her arm so tightly that she started to whimper, she had never seen his strong face display such terror. She followed his gaze and spotted a cluster of trees.

Something lay at the foot of the dark tree trunks.

Reinhardt was speechless. She was not used to this, he was always the one who took action, who would have something to say about every situation. She stared at the bundle at the foot of the trees, it was slim and white. She was struck by the awful thought that this might be a small person.

'It's a little kid,' Reinhardt whispered. He still did not move. Nor did he let go of her arm; his grip was vice-like.

'For Christ's sake, it's a little kid,' he repeated.

'No,' she said. Because it could not possibly be true, not here, not in Linde Forest.

Reinhardt took a step forward. He was no longer in any doubt, he could see arms and legs. A T-shirt with some writing on it. Kristine clasped her mouth. They stood like this for what seemed an eternity. The bundle lay immobile on the green moss. Kristine looked up at Reinhardt, her green eyes desperately pleading with him to do something.

'We must call the police!' she whispered.

Reinhardt started walking towards the cluster of trees, his body exuding reluctance. Ten paces, fifteen, they saw a foot and a fragile neck. It was a boy. He was lying on his stomach, he was naked from the waist down, and between his legs they could see blood, which had coagulated into rust-coloured scabs.

Kristine turned away in horror. But she could only look away for a few seconds. She had to look again, those green eyes had to see everything. The boy's short hair, his T-shirt with 'Kiss' written on it. The soles of his feet, pale pink against the dark moss.

'We have to call the police,' she whispered. 'We have to call the police now!'

Then she lost control of her body and started to shake. First her hands, then her shoulders. She had nothing to hold on to so she stumbled.

Reinhardt reached under her armpits and helped her back to her feet.

'Calm down now, calm down!' But she was unable to calm down. Inside her head she was issuing commands which never reached her arms and legs.

'112,' she whispered. 'You need to call 112.'

He quickly reached into his pocket for his mobile. 'You're sure it's not 113?'

She protested weakly, her body was rebelling: '112,' she repeated. 'The police!'

He entered the number at breakneck speed, started walking up and down while throwing quick glances at the dead body.

'We're calling from Linde Forest,' she heard him say. 'We're thirty minutes from the lake. We've found a small boy.'

Then he was silent for a few seconds, pressing the mobile against his ear.

'Yes, my name's Ris. Reinhardt Ris, we've been out for a walk. We've found a dead boy. You need to send someone.'

Again silence. Kristine gave in to the shaking, she sank down on to her knees and pressed her hands against the earth for support.

'No, there's no pulse,' Reinhardt shouted. 'Of course I'm sure. We can see that he's dead, he's gone all white!'

He came over to her, stopped, the sandy-coloured tuft stuck out.

'Yes, we can walk back to the barrier, our car's parked there, we'll wait for you.'

With considerable effort Kristine managed to stand up, and she started walking towards the edge of the clearing. Someone had stacked logs in a large pile and she slumped on to a log. She sat there watching the husband she knew inside out. Because she did, didn't she? Didn't she know every fibre of his powerful body, all his moods and his strong, commanding nature? He stood for a long time staring helplessly in every direction, a large man between the trees. All the qualities she normally associated with him sparkled by their absence. Authority, assurance and calm. Will and determination. It seemed as though he was prevaricating. She saw him walk back to the boy, saw him kneel down, he lowered his head and raised his hands to his face. What's he doing? she thought, baffled, is he crying, is that possible? Is he sitting there sobbing like a child? Have I misjudged him all these years, is he, in fact, a sensitive and emotional man?

Then the truth dawned on her.

He was taking pictures of the dead boy with his mobile.

CHAPTER 4

'How could you!' she screamed, outraged.

Her usual subservience had evaporated, gone was the fear of antagonising him, her limit had been reached and there was no holding her back.

She was crying and wiping away her tears, she half ran all the way to the barrier, but it took her a while because her legs were so short.

'You're insane!' she yelled.

Reinhardt scrambled behind her on the path, muffled swearwords reached her ears. They made it to the car simultaneously; Kristine slumped across the bonnet and sobbed. It was all too much for her: the body of the boy they had found and Reinhardt taking pictures of him. Reinhardt got into the car, found a cigarette and lit it, his lips tightened. Nevertheless Kristine thought she had detected a hint of embarrassment because she had pointed out his desire for sensation, something he would never own up to. He exhaled three times, the smoke coming out as white clouds.

'It was just a gut reaction,' he said, 'or, I don't know. It just happened.'

'But what do you want them for?'

She straightened up and looked at him, her green eyes shining. 'What are you going to do with those photos?'

'Nothing,' he replied in a sullen voice and kept smoking in defiance.

'Think about his parents,' she appealed to him. 'Imagine if they knew you had those photos: you have to delete them, it's not right!'

'Well, they don't know that I've got them,' he argued, slowly starting to get riled. 'And of course I'll delete them, I'm not an idiot, Kristine, how dare you take that tone with me, I'm in charge of my own life, so don't you start telling me what to do!'

When his outburst had finished, he carried on smoking. Kristine tried to calm herself down; she

16

was always terrified when he raised his voice. She was still slumped over the bonnet, feeling upset and nauseous. They peered down the road for the cars, which were meant to turn up. Kristine suddenly remembered something, she looked at Reinhardt in the car.

'That man we passed,' she said, 'the one we met at the barrier. In the blue anorak. What do you think he was doing up here?'

Reinhardt got out of the car and squatted down.

'It might have been him,' she said. 'He could barely look me in the eye. Surely we need to report him? They'll be asking us. If we saw anything. People or cars.'

Reinhardt coughed to clear his throat. He suddenly became very busy. He slammed the car door hard and started pacing up and down like he always did when he was in a state about something.

'The car?' he said. 'You saw the car?'

'Yes,' she said. 'I saw it quite clearly.'

'It was white,' he stated.

'It was an older model,' she said, 'but the paintwork was in very good condition.'

'We need to focus,' Reinhardt said. 'They'll want details.'

Kristine thought back. She had got a good look at the man, she had looked him in the eye, and an image of his face had imprinted itself on her retina. She had flashed him a brief smile out of reflex politeness, a smile he had not returned. He had looked back at her in horror and he had certainly behaved in a suspicious manner, as if they had caught him red-handed. I didn't like him, she thought, the one second I looked him in the eye was enough to give me a feeling about him, and it

17

was not a good one.

'How old was he?' Reinhardt said. 'What do you think, Kristine? Come on, we need to be ready.'

She thought carefully. 'Somewhere between forty and fifty,' she declared.

He wrinkled his nose with displeasure. 'We need to be more specific than that,' he stated. 'No, not as old as fifty.'

She made no reply. She, too, started pacing up and down the road, she circled their parked car. The sun shone off the silver Rover. Reinhardt made sure it was always washed and polished.

'I hope they get here soon,' she said.

'There'll be a whole army of them, Kristine, believe you me.'

She turned away from him and kept silent. She stuck her thumb in her mouth and chewed on a nail, a bad habit she had never managed to quit. Time had never passed so slowly, waiting had never felt like this. She could no longer enjoy the serenity of the forest, the susurration of the enormous treetops, the rustling leaves. She looked at Reinhardt for a long time. He was leaning against the car, his arms folded across his chest.

'What the hell is taking them so long?' he snapped.

'It's the road,' she replied. 'It's in poor condition. You can't drive very fast on it.'

They spoke no more. In their minds they were back by the cluster of trees, with the little boy, and Kristine was suddenly glad about the way he lay. Face down in the moss. She had not seen his eyes. She stared along the road. Finally she heard a car. Reinhardt stubbed out his cigarette and straightened his back. It was as if he was getting

18

ready for the performance of his life.

CHAPTER 5

A tall, grey-haired man led the solemn group. He
walked with a characteristic spring in his step and
made good use of his eyes; he watched Reinhardt
and Kristine, he took in the surroundings. Behind
him walked a younger man with an impressive
head of blond curls.

'That took you long enough,' Reinhardt started
off. 'I was the one who called you, my name's Ris,
Reinhardt Ris. He's lying right by the clearing over
there, by those trees. It's only a few minutes' walk.'

He turned and pointed in between the trees.
'Like I said, it's a small boy. He's lying face down,
he's half naked. We're in complete shock. We
come here every Sunday, we have done for many
years, but little did we think that we would ever
stumble across something like that and we don't
know what's happened, but I must admit that I'm
prepared for the worst, and I suppose you must be,
too. He's not all that old, either, six or seven
perhaps. Or what do you think, Kristine, is he as
old as seven?'

Reinhardt's cascade of words ceased. The grey-
haired man looked at him with narrow eyes, his
handshake was crushing. He introduced himself as
Konrad Sejer. While he shook Reinhardt's hand,
he looked at Kristine and his face softened. She
was relieved that someone was taking control. A
feeling of embarrassment brought colour to her
cheeks, she did not understand why, but it had

19

something to do with his eyes and his presence.

'You both found him?' he asked.

'Reinhardt spotted him first,' Kristine said.

'Are you finding this hard?'

'Yes,' she admitted, 'it's hard.'

He nodded. 'It's good that there are two of you, it's easier when you've got someone to share it with.'

We haven't shared anything for ages, she thought despondently.

'We saw a man,' Reinhardt interjected. 'A man leaving, he was in a hurry. We passed him at the barrier; he drove off in a white car. He drove off at speed.'

Sejer's eyebrows lifted one millimetre; he rarely displayed stronger expressions than that. In the younger detective's face there was a hint of a smile as he became aware of Reinhardt's need for attention.

'We managed to get quite a few details,' Reinhardt said. 'We had only just parked, we walked past him at close range.'

Sejer nodded calmly.

Kristine started walking. She felt a resistance inside her and she dreaded it. The curly-haired detective came up to her, stuck out his hand and introduced himself as Jacob Skarre. He reminded her a bit of a gangly teenager with huge, bright blue eyes and curls that any girl would envy him. Behind him followed a group of crime scene officers carrying equipment needed at the scene of the murder. Or where they had found the body, Kristine thought. Without knowing why, she was absolutely certain that the boy had been killed elsewhere and later brought here by the killer. She

20

thought about the man at the barrier and she shuddered as she recalled his disturbed eyes.

*　　*　　*

She sat on one of the logs as the crime scene officers started their painstaking work. She watched them as they carefully took their places. She was finally overcome by a sense of calm, now that everyone had a job to do she saw no signs of horror, only gravity. But as soon as she started to think about it, she was gripped by despair because the boy had parents, and they did not know yet. They might be sharing a joke right now. She could visualise them clearly in their living room, perhaps the sun was streaming in through the window. The image took her breath away.

Her thoughts were interrupted by Reinhardt's voice cutting through the silence, it was loud and self-assured. She was so fed up with his voice; she was mortified that he could not keep his mouth shut. The inspector and his colleague had both knelt down, shoulder by shoulder, in the heather. Now they would see what she had seen, the details which would reveal what had happened to the boy. Reinhardt suddenly came over to her. Perhaps they had told him to move back, she wondered, as she looked up.

'Have you realised something?' he asked, sitting down beside her.

'No,' she said in a drained voice.

'Something's missing.'

She gave him a perplexed look. 'What's that?'

'The press,' he said, as if he were an expert in these things.

21

Her eyes widened.

'Thank God for that,' she exclaimed.

'*VG* magazine would pay thousands for a story like this.'

He looked at her.

'You can't call them,' she said. 'You can't!'

'But for God's sake, think about it. They're going to be all over this story anyway.'

'Not if you keep your mouth shut.'

'This will be on the news by the evening,' he said, 'and that's only right and proper, in my opinion. People should be given the chance to protect their kids; that boy over there, he's only six or seven.'

She made no reply. Her lips had narrowed and she looked tormented.

'We need to go down to the station,' she whispered. 'We need to make a statement.'

'I know.'

'What if we remember it wrong? We mustn't say something unless we're sure.'

'You remember a little,' he said, 'and so do I. He won't get away with it.'

Kristine shook her head. 'He might just have been out for a walk,' she said. 'Like we were.'

*   *   *

Snorrason, the pathologist, rolled the boy on to his back. Now they could see his face and his half-open eyes.

'I've authorised overtime, Skarre,' Sejer said.

Skarre nodded grimly.

'I'll work day and night on this,' he said.

Snorrason worked with gentle, gloved hands.

22

'He's such a little lad,' he said quietly, shaking his strawberry-blond head.

'His mother might already have reported him missing,' Sejer said. 'Check with the station, Jacob.'

Skarre stood up and turned his back to the others.

'No visible lesions,' Snorrason said. 'No cuts or needle marks. No signs of strangulation, no effusions of the eyeballs. No signs of a struggle, no defensive injuries.'

Sejer looked at the pale-faced boy.

'He might have used a pillow,' Snorrason said, 'or something else he might have had to hand. A coat, or a blanket.'

'Would you be able to tell if he had used a pillow?' Sejer asked.

'Not necessarily. There is no evidence of pressure to the face. Often you'll find a linear impression from the teeth on the inside of the lips, but he doesn't have that.'

'What else can you tell me?'

Snorrason opened the boy's mouth and looked inside.

'Caucasian boy aged eight to nine. Short and very slender. I estimate he weighs between twenty-five and thirty kilos. He's missing a tooth in his upper jaw. And,' here he looked up at Sejer, 'he's bitten his tongue deeply.'

Sejer listened without displaying any sign of emotion.

'Evidence suggests he was sexually assaulted,' Snorrason continued, 'but he shows no signs of other types of abuse. In other words, I don't know why he died.'

23

Sejer had to stand up, his knees were about to give way; he watched Skarre, who was on his mobile. Then he watched the couple waiting on the log. The man was blatantly staring at them, the woman stabbed at the heather with a stick. Skarre put his mobile back in his pocket.

'Anything?' Sejer asked.

'Duty officer received a call at two this afternoon. A mother in Huseby reported her son missing, he had slept over at a friend's house and was meant to walk home this morning. She has called everyone she can think of, and she has given us a description of his clothes.'

'And?' Sejer waited.

'It's very likely to be him,' Skarre said. 'Jonas August Løwe. Turns eight next month. Small and skinny with short, blond hair. He was wearing a black T-shirt with the word 'Kiss' on it. Red Bermuda shorts. White, brand new trainers. Have we found his shorts or his trainers?'

'No.'

Sejer took a few steps across the heather. He repeated the name to himself. The low sun made his grey hair glow. His face was still motionless, but it was possible for those who knew him well to detect a minute tightening of his jaw. He headed towards the waiting couple. Reinhardt Ris looked up at him in a rather direct manner.

'As I mentioned,' Sejer said, 'we'll need you to come down to the station.'

Reinhardt leapt up from the log and stood to attention before the inspector.

'Please go to your car,' Sejer said. 'Skarre and I will follow. Drive to the station, go to the reception area and wait.'

24

They walked briskly back to the barrier. Their lives will never be the same, Sejer thought, an experience like this will knock them off their course. They both showed signs of it, the man by exaggerating his own masculinity, the woman by stumbling helplessly after him. He watched them for a while as he reflected on this. Then he quickly walked back to Jonas August Løwe.

CHAPTER 6

The police station towered over the busy street, a colossus of glass and red-brown stone. High up on its façade hung the emblem of the police force, its metal gleaming in the sunshine. Its architecture signalled power and authority. Reinhardt opened the glass door and entered, Kristine hurrying after him. The reception was a large, open area with a circular, dark-varnished counter, behind which a woman gave them a questioning look. The blue glare from a computer monitor drained her face of colour.

'Can I help you?' she asked.

'We're waiting for Konrad Sejer,' Reinhardt said.

They were directed to a sofa. Reinhardt started drumming his fingers on the armrest. The receptionist returned to her monitor, Kristine peeled off her red coat.

'Looks like we could be here for some time,' Reinhardt moaned.

'I don't mind staying here all night,' Kristine said. 'I wouldn't be able to do anything else anyway. Washing clothes, cooking dinner, it all seems so unimportant now.'

Reinhardt got up and crossed the floor. He stared impatiently out of the windows. He pulled his mobile out of his pocket, turning his back on her as he did so.

'What are you doing?' she asked anxiously.

'Sending a text message.'

She followed him nervously with her eyes. There was an air of excitement about him, she recognised it from earlier occasions. When he got a tax rebate of forty thousand kroner, when they bought the car, the silver Rover. The manner in which he had swaggered into the car showroom, like a bowlegged sailor. She hated this side to his personality, that he always had to show off, and her loathing grew with every passing year. Then she tried looking at it from a different point of view, a positive angle because he was her husband and she wanted to be generous. He was a faithful and hard-working man with well-built shoulders and coarse, sandy hair. His face was broad and strong, his thighs were muscular and rock hard. When she walked down the street with him, sometimes other women would turn to check him out. Her being so petite and him being so much taller than her had once appealed to her, she felt sheltered like a child. He was her protector; he was the one who dealt with things. Sometimes, out of the blue, he would turn into a big kid, lift her high in the air and be loving. Then she warmed to him again, became happy almost and once more she would put up with him. So it oscillated inside her and this duality was a source of immense confusion to her.

Finally he put away his mobile. He sat down and

sighed deeply.

'Well,' he said, 'at least we'll have something to talk about now.'

'All we did was find a little boy,' she said quietly.

She did not look him in the eye, she was talking to her lap.

'But it's not a straightforward case,' Reinhardt said, 'of murder. I mean, first he did something else to him, well, I can't even say it out loud, and afterwards he killed him.'

'We don't know how he died,' she objected.

'Kristine,' he said in an exasperated voice. 'Don't tell me you haven't worked out what's happened here? Come on, what do you take me for?'

Reinhardt had found himself in an extraordinary situation. He had been the first person to arrive at a crime scene. Furthermore, he had observed a man at a distance of only a few metres, a man who was leaving. He regarded himself as significant and important. Kristine could please herself, but there was no way she was going to tell him how to handle the situation. Again he got up from the sofa and wandered around restlessly. The woman behind the counter trailed him with her eyes.

Finally, Sejer and Skarre arrived at reception, the door groaning shut behind them. Reinhardt and Kristine followed them noiselessly down the corridors on the green carpet. Kristine kept rewinding time, the images returned in fragments. She saw the man in the blue anorak, she recalled his car door slamming and his engine revving, grit and gravel spouting from underneath the tyres. What had she thought, what had she felt? That they had disturbed him? I can't tell them that, she

27

thought, that's subjective. They're looking for accurate, factual observations, I can't speculate. Sejer and Skarre remained silent, but they walked as if they belonged together, as if they were a couple, she thought, as if they had grown accustomed to each other. There was trust between them.

They reached Sejer's office. Kristine entered, cradling her red coat. In the midst of this anonymous glass, stone and concrete building was a large, bright office with colourful curtains. She noticed individual details: a stately chair with a tall back, a lamp with a yellow shade and underneath it, a clumsy figure made from salt dough. The ravages of time had caused the figure to grow mouldy, but there was no doubt that it represented a police officer in a blue uniform. On the desk was a laminated desk pad with a map of the world; a pen covered Italy and the coastline of Tunisia. There were photographs on the walls. A man, who looked like Sejer, with a dog. A dark-skinned teenage boy. On a table there were some plants, there was a cupboard, and several red ring binders on a shelf. Criminal cases, she thought, human tragedies. Death and despair. The boy they had found would probably get his own space on the shelf. He would become one of the red binders.

'Do you know who he is?' she whispered. 'The boy, I mean?'

'We think so,' Sejer said.

She folded her hands in her lap. She looked like a shy schoolgirl waiting for permission to speak.

'You saw a man by the barrier,' Sejer said. 'We need a description, because we want to talk to him. What can you tell us about the clothes he wore, his

28

appearance, his age?'

'He was tall,' Reinhardt said. 'One metre eighty-five, I would say.'

Kristine shook her head. 'No,' she said, 'he wasn't that tall. He was much shorter than you, Reinhardt.'

Sejer looked at them calmly. 'Let's not worry about centimetres,' he said affably. 'What was he wearing?'

'A windbreaker,' Reinhardt said. 'Dark blue.'

'An anorak,' Kristine corrected him. 'The old-fashioned type with a drawstring hem and a cord around the waist. It had a Norwegian flag on one shoulder. The left shoulder,' she added, touching her own shoulder.

'He wore white trousers,' Reinhardt said.

'No,' said Kristine, 'they were beige. With multiple pockets on the thighs. He was wearing trainers, brown ones. They were quite old and in hideous condition.'

Jacob Skarre made notes.

'How old was he?' Sejer asked.

'Forty-something, we think,' Reinhardt said.

'Build?'

'It was like I said,' Reinhardt stated. 'He was tall and slim.'

Kristine looked up at Sejer.

'It's true that he was slim,' she said. 'I mean, he wasn't fat or overweight. But he was broad. If you know what I mean. Across the hips.'

Reinhardt narrowed his lips.

'Did you get a look at his face?'

'He looked stressed,' Reinhardt said. 'We agree on that, don't we, Kristine?'

His question sounded like a command.

29

Sejer looked at Kristine. 'What do you think? Was he stressed?'

'He might just have been shy, but he was startled when he saw us. Then again, he would be, wouldn't he, we appeared so suddenly,' she explained.

'Anything else?'

'He had light blond hair,' Reinhardt said.

'No,' Kristine contradicted him, 'his hair was grey. It had been combed back and it was quite long in the neck. Slightly curly,' she added.

'What about his car?' Sejer asked.

'It was white,' Kristine said, 'and quite old.'

'I've been thinking about that car,' Reinhardt said. 'It might have been a Granada.' He sent Kristine a triumphant look. This was outside her area of expertise.

'A Granada? I don't think there are many of those around these days, we'll need to look into that. What do you think, Kristine?' Sejer asked.

'I don't know anything about cars,' she mumbled.

'But, all the same, it was a large passenger car. A four-door saloon?'

'Yes,' said Reinhardt.

'So he saw you and drove off?'

'In a hell of a rush,' Reinhardt said.

'I don't think he drove off that quickly,' Kristine objected.

Now it was Skarre's turn to smile.

'Did either of you see the number plate?' he asked optimistically.

They were both silent.

'Anyway,' Sejer said, 'it wasn't a man you recognised, I mean you haven't seen this man before?'

30

'No.'

Sejer pondered this for a while. He moved the pen from Tunisia further south into Africa.

'Did you notice anything else unusual on your walk from the barrier to the lake? Any people? Sounds, voices?'

'Nothing,' Reinhardt said. 'There wasn't a soul around and it was quiet. Linde Forest is always really quiet.'

'That's why we go there,' Kristine interjected.

'And going there in your car, before you parked, did you meet anyone? Did you pass any other cars, people out walking?'

Reinhardt had to think about this.

'Did we pass anyone?' He looked at Kristine.

'No,' she said. 'The road's so narrow that if we'd met anyone, we would have had to stop.'

'You often walk there? It's a favourite walk of yours?'

'Every Sunday after lunch,' Kristine said, 'usually about the same time. Whatever the weather. All year round.'

'Have you noticed anything else unusual up there, on previous visits?'

'No. Like I said, it's really quiet there. We might have seen the odd person berry-picking. And skiers in winter. But you have to walk all the way to the lake from the barrier and most people can't be bothered to do that.'

'This man,' Sejer said, 'would you recognise him if you saw him in the street?'

'Yes,' Kristine said quickly.

'Why are you so certain?'

She hesitated. 'He stood out.'

Sejer pricked up his ears.

31

'In what way?'

She thought about the face she had seen for only a few brief seconds.

'I'm not making this up,' she said, 'but he reminded me of someone.' She rubbed her mouth nervously.

'And who did he remind you of?'

Her reply was barely audible. 'Hans Christian Andersen,' she whispered.

The office fell silent.

'The writer, you mean? What made him look like Hans Christian Andersen?' Sejer asked.

'His low, sloping forehead,' she said. 'His huge nose and large ears. The high cheekbones and crescent of curly hair at the back of his neck.'

Reinhardt sent her a doubting look. Skarre was busy taking notes.

'You shouldn't pay too much attention to what I say,' Kristine added. 'It was just something that crossed my mind.'

Sejer got up from his chair. 'That, too, can be important. That'll be all for now. Go home and relax. As much as you can.'

'Are we done?' Reinhardt asked in surprise.

Sejer gave him a patient look.

'Unless you happen to remember something you think might be important,' he said, 'in which case I'd be grateful if you'd call me.'

Skarre escorted them out into the corridor. Suddenly Kristine seemed to remember something. She clasped her mouth and gave them a wide-eyed look.

'Good God,' she said.

'What is it?' Skarre asked.

'Please forgive me,' she said, 'I'm not quite

32

myself. And neither is Reinhardt. We forgot the most important thing, I don't know how we managed that. He was limping,' she added.

'That's right,' Reinhardt exclaimed.

'Or rather,' Kristine went on, 'he might not have been limping. But he was walking differently, as if he had an injury of some sort.'

Skarre nodded. 'A disability?'

'Or,' Reinhardt said, 'he might have had a false leg.'

CHAPTER 7

'If I had my way,' Sejer said, 'we would be out questioning every convicted paedophile in the area. Even the ones who have been charged, but never convicted due to lack of evidence.'

'The courts will never give us the green light to do that,' Skarre said.

'Then we run a red light,' Sejer said. 'We run a red light and we pay the price.'

'What do you make of Mr and Mrs Ris?'

'Kristine Ris is a keen observer,' Sejer declared, 'and women make better witnesses than men. They pay attention to details, the little things. A glance or a mood. The Hans Christian Andersen comment was interesting; it was remarkable that she made that observation. Andersen looked unusual; do you know what he looked like?'

'No.'

'He wasn't particularly attractive,' Sejer said. 'If I remember rightly, there was something fox-like about him.'

33

'Fox-like how?'

'Oh, it's just my impression. But I don't think his appearance reflected his creative powers.'

'The Ugly Duckling,' Skarre suggested.

'Exactly.'

Sejer walked over to the window, he stared out into the busy street.

'What's the name of Jonas August's mother? Did you make a note of it?'

'Her name's Elfrid,' Skarre said, 'Elfrid Løwe. She lives on Granatveien in Huseby. Do you want to call ahead? Do you want to let her know that we're coming over?'

'She'll be at home,' he replied, 'she'll be waiting. Come on, let's go.'

'You don't want to call the local vicar?'

'No.'

'Why not?' Skarre asked.

'Because I'm better at this.'

As he spoke, the doubts came. What could he actually tell her? We've found a little boy by Lake Linde. He matches your description of Jonas August and we need you to come with us to the Institute of Forensic Medicine first thing tomorrow morning, so we can confirm whether or not the dead boy is your son. Those would be his words. And in one second her life would go from order to chaos.

'You go and start the car,' he said.

Skarre grabbed his jacket and left. Sejer wandered around his office. He studied the photos on the wall of Ingrid, his daughter, and her son, Matteus, a tall, athletic teenager. He stood there looking at them, reminding himself of the magnitude of losing those closest to you. He could

34

not articulate it, but for obvious reasons he would have to find the words. Elfrid Løwe would look him in the eye and demand an explanation.

* * *

She saw them from the window.

She ran out of the house immediately. Sejer walked across the gravel with heavy, measured steps. It was his slow pace that confirmed her worst fears.

'Elfrid Løwe?'

She ignored his outstretched hand. Instead she clung to the fence.

'Could we come inside, please?' Sejer asked.

She shook her head in defiance. She was slender and small like her son and she wore a short turquoise and pink dress with a floral pattern. She began picking nervously at a ribbon on the neckline of the dress. Her hands were lean with clearly visible veins.

'I want to hear it right here,' she said. 'I want to know right now.'

She shook her head again.

'So tell me,' she burst out, 'please tell me what's happened!'

Sejer placed a hand on her arm. 'I want you to go inside and sit down.'

Finally she went back inside the house. She stood on the living room floor shifting her weight from one foot to the other in a nervous, rhythmical movement.

'Sit down, please,' Sejer told her.

His authoritative voice made her sit on the sofa.

'We have found a little boy,' he started, 'in Linde

Forest, not far from the lake. He's been dead a few hours. And I'm so sorry to have to tell you this, but he matches your description of Jonas August.'

'No,' she said, shaking her head. 'No.'

'We think it's him,' Sejer said.

She continued shaking her head. She looked like a sullen child who has been thwarted.

'We'll take him to the Institute of Forensic Medicine in Oslo tomorrow morning,' Sejer said. 'You'll need to come with us and together we will see him.'

'Tomorrow?' she said blankly. Her hands scrambled across the coffee table. 'But where is he now? Where will he be tonight?' She lifted one hand and bit into her knuckles while she waited for a response. She stared at Skarre now, her eyes demanding a reply.

'We haven't been able to move him yet,' Skarre said.

'You haven't been able to move him? I don't understand.'

'We need to examine the crime scene and the surrounding area,' Skarre said. 'It takes time, we won't be able to finish this evening. So we'll be working through the night.'

She punched the air wildly with her fists.

'You can't come here telling me he has to stay in the forest all night,' she screamed. 'For God's sake, he's only seven years old!'

'I'm afraid he has to,' Skarre said. 'The crime scene officers haven't finished.'

'No,' she protested, 'you have to take him to a hospital, so he'll have a bed! There are animals up there and it'll be cold at night and I just won't allow it.' She leapt up from the sofa and howled. 'I

36

won't allow it!'

Sejer stood up, but she refused to be calmed down.

'We have a lot of work ahead of us, Elfrid,' he said. 'It's vital for us to find the man who did this as quickly as possible. I give you my word that he won't be lying there on his own. Our people will be guarding him the whole time.'

'We've put up a tent,' Skarre explained, 'there's light and heating.'

She hid her mouth with one hand.

'Why didn't I go to meet him?' she whispered. 'I can't bear it. I should have walked down to meet him and none of this would have happened. He's only seven years old, I should have known that something might happen, I should have known!'

Her words turned into terrified sobs.

'What about his father?' Sejer asked. 'Jonas August's father. Does he live here with you?'

She shook her head.

'We don't talk to him.'

'It would be best if you would call him,' Sejer said, 'so he can come with us tomorrow morning to the Institute of Forensic Medicine. At least you'll have each other.'

'We were never a couple,' she said. Again she picked at the ribbon on her dress. She had short blonde hair, she looked like a teenage boy in girls' clothing.

'I have no idea where he is, he doesn't know about Jonas. He left me before I had time to tell him I was pregnant. Jonas is a secret.'

'So there's no one we can contact?' Sejer asked.

'Why do you think it's Jonas?' she asked.

'His clothes,' Skarre explained.

'But all boys wear T-shirts and shorts, they all wear the same things and it's been a warm day. Are you telling me that the boy up at Linde Forest is wearing a T-shirt and red shorts?'

Skarre thought about the shorts, which they still had not found. He fought a silent battle trying to decide how much information to give her.

'We think it's Jonas,' he said.

She grew angry and her cheeks became flushed. 'Was he wearing red shorts?'

Skarre looked straight into her eyes. It cost him a great deal.

'We haven't found his shorts,' he conceded.

'You haven't found his shorts? But surely he was wearing them?'

A hint of suspicion emerged in her face. Skarre struggled to find the right words, the ones he would have to say out loud.

'The boy we found wasn't wearing any shorts,' he admitted.

Elfrid Løwe paled. The men watched as her imagination ran riot.

'We really don't want to speculate as to what might have happened,' Sejer said calmly. 'It remains to be seen. But we need to be honest with you. We have good reasons to fear that the dead boy is Jonas. I want you to prepare yourself for that. But when it comes to what happened to him, we shouldn't guess.'

'Perhaps you've made a mistake,' she said, biting her knuckle once more. 'And this might just be a routine visit. It could be, couldn't it?' Her eyes pleaded with them; they were dark blue like Jonas August's.

'Yes,' Sejer said reluctantly.

38

'And this boy,' she asked again, 'the boy you've found. How did he die?'

'We don't know yet.'

'But when will you know? How long will I have to wait?'

'Until the autopsy report is ready.'

'You intend to carry out an autopsy on him?'

'We have to in cases like this.'

'That means you'll have to cut him,' she gasped.

'An autopsy is an important piece of work which is essential to our investigation,' Skarre explained and realised as soon as he had spoken how insensitive his words sounded.

'I know what it means,' she screamed. 'Jonas will be cut open and all his organs will be removed and replaced with newspaper, so he'll be lying in his coffin stuffed with rubbish and I'll have to live with that for the rest of my life. My little boy stuffed full of rubbish!'

She buried her face in her hands. Skarre feared that she was going to have a nervous breakdown.

'The most important thing we can do for him now is find out what happened to him,' he said.

'Can I withhold my consent?' she whispered. 'Can I stop the autopsy?'

'Not in a case like this,' Sejer said. 'The autopsy will provide us with crucial information. Besides,' he added, and he hated having to say it, 'there are other considerations to take into account. Other children might be at risk. Do you understand?'

She nodded.

'Is there someone you would like us to call?' he asked.

'Not until we're sure,' she whispered. 'You might have made a mistake and I don't want to worry my

39

friends unnecessarily. Or my parents, they won't be able to handle it. They're not very well, my father's got a weak heart and my mother's got Parkinson's. They won't be able to cope with this,' she said. 'I don't care what you say, but I choose to believe that you've made a mistake. There are lots of those T-shirts, they sell them everywhere. We'll drive up to Linde Forest, we'll go right now, I have to see him, you can't deny me that, he's my Jonas and I'm in charge!'

She had got up from the sofa and was heading for the hall; her desperation had taken over.

'I'm sorry,' Sejer said firmly, following her. 'I can't allow that.'

She started to scream. She came back into the living room, staggered to an armchair, slumped over it and howled.

'So I'm supposed to just go to bed tonight knowing that he's lying in the forest with no shorts on?' she sobbed. 'I can't believe that you're allowed to do this, I want to talk to someone else!'

'Elfrid,' Skarre said, 'we're on your side!'

She emitted some feeble sobs.

'We have family support officers who can help you,' Sejer said. 'If you want them.'

'No,' she whispered. 'No, I'm going to lie in my bed.'

'If you need a sedative, we can arrange for that.'

'Don't want one.'

She gave them a defiant stare.

'You've probably made a mistake,' she stated. 'There's always a chance.'

She smiled and held her head high. 'There's always a chance.'

CHAPTER 8

People everywhere were talking about Jonas August Løwe.

In the corridors of the Central Hospital, at the hairdresser's, in cabs, on the buses, in cafés and shops. In front rooms and back rooms, in waiting rooms and offices. They talked about Jonas on the stairs and in hallways. Two inmates were sitting on a bench in the exercise yard behind the county jail.

'They're bound to catch him,' one of them said, 'and this is where he'll end up. And when he gets here, we'll know what to do with him.'

'Bloody right, we will,' said the other.

A press conference was held at the station. Sejer had never had much time for the police's duty to inform the general public and he regarded journalists as sharks: one drop of blood and they all came rushing. But as always he behaved impeccably as he briefed the press. Jonas August was a Year Three pupil at Solberg School. He lived with his mother and he was an only child. A couple had observed a man not far from the crime scene, a man approximately fifty years old and wearing a blue anorak. Jonas was partly dressed and he appeared to have been sexually assaulted. As yet it was unclear where and how he had died, whether his death had occurred where he was found or whether he had been killed elsewhere and brought there later. All available manpower would be assigned to the case with immediate effect, and they would also summon any available outside expertise. When asked if the killer might strike

41

again, he looked at them gravely and replied, 'We have no reason to think anything like that.'

'Do we need to take extra care of our children?'

'We always need to take care of our children.'

'What are you going to do now?'

'We have a procedure and we'll follow it.'

They wanted to know what he thought of the crime scene. Wasn't it strange that the boy had not been buried or concealed in some way?

'Perhaps he wanted us to find him quickly,' Sejer said.

'But he might have buried him. You would have lost valuable time and the killer would have had the advantage. In a few months it'll start snowing and everything will freeze over.'

'It wouldn't have been an advantage,' Sejer said, 'merely a delay.'

He talked and he talked and he experienced an odd feeling of being split in two. Half of him behaved like the professional he was; the other half observed. The faces in the briefing room, the solemn mood, a fly scuttling across the table before eventually settling on the microphone stand.

'Will you be talking to convicted sex offenders?'

'According to the law we can only question people if we have reasonable grounds to suspect them.'

'Did you make any interesting discoveries at the crime scene?'

'I don't wish to comment on that.'

'The man who was seen by the barrier. Was he behaving suspiciously?'

'No comment.'

'Has your force previously investigated a case of this nature?'

'No, we haven't.'

'So are you saying you're wandering into uncharted territory?'

'No.'

'How long had the boy been dead before he was found?'

'We're talking about a few hours, according to the Institute of Forensic Medicine.'

'Is there anything about this case which makes it unique?'

At this point Sejer got up to signal that the briefing was over.

'Every case is unique,' he said. 'There was only ever one Jonas August.'

CHAPTER 9

Sejer's office chair was made by Kinnarps, and Sejer had paid for it out of his own pocket. It had a steel frame, a seat which could be raised and lowered, the back reclined, and a button made the chair rock backwards and forwards. Sejer loathed rocking, however, and consequently never touched it. Underneath his desk lay his dog, Frank Robert, a Chinese Shar Pei, his wrinkled head resting heavily on his paws. He had the same temperament as his fellow countrymen; he was both inscrutable and dignified. In addition he never barked, but might occasionally emit a disgruntled snort. Sejer tapped in the number for the Institute of Forensic Medicine and asked for Snorrason. When he heard his voice, he was instantly reminded of the caramel-like smell of the tobacco that always surrounded him.

'How far have you got?' he asked.

'I'm well under way,' Snorrason replied, 'and though much is still unclear, I can tell you the following: the boy died as a result of oxygen deprivation.'

'So we're talking about strangulation?'

'This is where it gets odd, because I can't work out how it happened. My findings are not conclusive, I need more time.'

'I'm not sure I understand you,' Sejer said. 'If he was deprived of oxygen surely it follows that someone deprived him of it? With a hand or a pillow. Or are you saying that he got something stuck in his throat?'

'No, he definitely didn't choke. And I can't make sense of it either,' Snorrason said, 'but I don't think it's what it looks like. I need to make some calls.'

'Who to?'

'Elfrid Løwe among others. I have a theory,' he said. 'I'll be in touch when I can prove it.'

'Have you found what we were hoping for most of all?'

'You're referring to DNA?'

'Yes?'

'Yes, I've found DNA evidence. If you find the perpetrator, we have irrefutable proof here.'

'Good,' Sejer said. 'Anything else?'

'Not at this moment in time. The boy doesn't even have a scratch on him, and they usually do.'

'Will you be able to finish the autopsy report tonight?'

'I'll fax it over later. You're welcome to wait for it.'

44

Sejer thanked him and hung up. He unbuttoned the cuff of his left shirt-sleeve and started scratching. He suffered from psoriasis and there was a red and irritated patch the size of a twenty-kroner coin on his elbow. He began reading the reports submitted so far. At regular intervals, he glanced sideways at the fax machine. Finally the telephone rang. It was Snorrason.

'I've spoken to Elfrid Løwe,' he said. 'Jonas August suffered from asthma.'

'Did he? Is that relevant?'

'The assault triggered a severe attack. And that, as far as I can establish, was what killed him.'

CHAPTER 10

Reinhardt and Kristine Ris's house was attractive and well maintained. It was painted white and had green windowsills and glazed Dutch roof tiles. It was built in 1920 and Reinhardt was fond of referring to it as an architectural pearl. It sat on a hill above the town and from the first floor veranda they could see the river with its many bridges that resembled broad stitches across a cut. Behind the house was a small garden surrounded by a neatly trimmed hedge; in front of the house a double garage and a swing installed by the previous owners. Kristine would sometimes gaze out of the window, pretending that her little girl was playing on it. But there was no little girl. The urge for a child dragged her down like a dead weight in the water.

She looked into the living room. Reinhardt was

45

sitting in front of the computer playing EverQuest. He was completely absorbed by the game, all Kristine saw was his broad, unapproachable back. She tried to open herself to him, open up what was good in him; he had traits she valued highly. But it was an uphill struggle. A sneaking reluctance crept in with increasing frequency and her lack of enthusiasm made her feel guilty, because she had promised to keep herself only unto him until death did them part. She noticed that he seemed restless, visibly tense, he kept looking at his watch, and every now and again he would glance out at the road as if he was expecting someone. Kristine found an old newspaper, put it on the dining table and started polishing a silver candelabra. She rubbed it with a cloth, hard and with practised ease. When she had finished polishing the candelabra, she would light a candle for Jonas August. She was not going to tell Reinhardt, he would not understand anyway, nor did he care much about her innermost thoughts. 'It has to be out in the open,' he would say. 'I can't be doing with guessing what's on people's minds.'

'Irmelin and Kjell are coming over,' he said out of the blue. He turned in the chair and looked at her, clearly anticipating protests.

'They'll be here in half an hour,' he added.

Kristine gave him a shocked look. 'In half an hour? And you're telling me that now?' Her eyes automatically scanned the room for anything that needed to be tidied away.

Reinhardt switched off his computer.'I invited them over for a drink,' he said.

'But why didn't you tell me?'

He went over to the sofa. He made himself

comfortable with the newspaper, spreading it out demonstratively on the coffee table.

'What's wrong with inviting a few friends over for a glass of wine?' he snapped.

'Nothing,' she said, 'but couldn't you have told me earlier? I've got nothing in the house, Reinhardt, nothing at all.'

He shook his head in exasperation. 'There's no need for food,' he said. 'We'll just offer them a glass of wine, that's enough. It's called having a nice time with your friends.'

She did not want to sound petty, and they had invited Kjell and Irmelin over before, but it had always been for dinner. Then she realised what this was really about. Reinhardt was dying to tell them his news, he had something to treat them to, and it was more than likely that he would drone on the whole night about Jonas August. He would bask in the limelight and she would feel ashamed. There was something about the way he was dealing with this which she despised, though whether or not her own approach was superior or nobler she found difficult to tell.

'You could have asked me,' she repeated, hurt. She resumed polishing the silver; she could see her face now in the base of the candelabra.

He rustled his newspaper angrily. 'I don't need your permission to invite a friend round,' he said. 'I live here too, it's my house.'

It's my house. As if he let her live there out of the goodness of his heart. She did not reply, her throat swelled up. She finished the candelabra and got a candle from a kitchen drawer, then she found a match and lit it, inhaling the comforting smell of burnt sulphur. She stood for a while gazing at the

47

restless flame.

'It's flickering,' she said. 'Look.'

Reinhardt looked up. 'Must be a draught somewhere.'

'There's no draught. Nothing is open.'

'Turn on the radio, please,' Reinhardt asked her. 'The news will be on soon. We need to find out if there have been any developments.'

She did as he had asked. A woman was reporting on the body found in Linde Forest.

'He was an only child,' Kristine whispered.

The thought saddened her. It meant that someone was left alone now, robbed of everything.

'A man wearing a blue anorak,' Reinhardt said, 'who was seen leaving in a pale car.' But we gave them so much more information. I mean, about how he was dressed. He was limping too, why didn't she say anything about that?'

Kristine shrugged. 'Well, he wasn't really limping,' she said. 'He just walked in an odd way. Perhaps we were mistaken, perhaps we can't rely on our memories. Besides,' she added, 'we disagreed about several things.'

'No,' he said firmly. 'We did not disagree and we are not mistaken. Nothing wrong up here,' he added, tapping his temple with his finger. He returned to his newspaper; that, too, was crammed with stories about Jonas August. Kristine let her head sink back against the headrest of her armchair, folded her hands in her lap and tried to relax. It was quiet until the doorbell rang in the hall. Reinhardt shot up from the sofa, Kristine remained in the armchair watching the flickering candle.

The guests entered the living room, smiling.

Irmelin held a potted plant in her hands, a small begonia. Reinhardt disappeared into the basement and returned with a three-litre box of Chablis.

'Get the glasses, Kristine, would you?' he called out. Their guests sat down at the table, Irmelin, dark and slender, Kjell, sturdy with thinning hair. He started talking about his job; he was a chiropractor and the others listened. A teenage girl had thrown up all over his coat because she could not bear the sound of bones cracking. A colleague was involved in some awful case where a woman had been paralysed from the waist down following treatment.

'And what about you?' he said eventually. 'Any news?'

He might as well have shone a spotlight on Reinhardt.

'Well,' Reinhardt said, 'something very dramatic has happened since we last saw you. You've probably heard it on the news.'

'Dramatic?' Kjell was baffled.

'Jonas August Løwe,' Reinhardt explained. 'The boy whose body was found up in Linde Forest.'

Once the case was mentioned all four turned serious and it was a long time before anyone said anything.

'He was found by a couple out walking,' Reinhardt explained. 'A couple who go walking to Lake Linde every Sunday.'

Kjell shook his head in disbelief. 'You don't mean that you were the ones who found him?'

Reinhardt planted his elbows on the table. 'Yes, indeed we were,' he said. 'And we've been questioned.'

'Why did they want to question you?' Kjell

49

asked.

'Because we saw a man up there and he was acting suspiciously, I'm certain of it. We passed him just by the barrier and now the police are looking for him. They say he is a witness, obviously, but that's what they always say. Personally, I thought he looked guilty as sin.'

'Perhaps he was just out for a walk, like you were,' Kjell suggested.

'But hardly anyone ever goes there,' Reinhardt objected. 'Besides, he looked very agitated.'

'So tell us more,' Irmelin begged.

'We had reached the lake,' he said, 'and were on our way back to the car. We were walking through the forest and there he was, lying on his stomach, face down. It wasn't difficult to see what had happened to him, if you know what I mean.'

He paused to let his words sink in and take effect.

'We couldn't believe our eyes,' he said. 'I called 112 and it took them twenty minutes to get up there. Kristine was shaking like a leaf.'

'But the man by the barrier,' Irmelin asked. 'Have you seen him before?'

'Never,' Reinhardt said.

'He was walking in a funny way,' Kristine said. 'I mean, he wasn't limping, but he was dragging one leg. When he walked he had to swing it in front of the other.'

'My guess is he has a false leg,' Reinhardt said. 'If he ends up in court, we'll probably have to give evidence.'

Kjell shook his head in disbelief. 'Well, that's what you'll be hoping for, I know you. For Christ's sake, Reinhardt, all you did was see a man in the forest. Get over yourself.'

'Perhaps we just startled him,' Kristine said. 'We did appear out of nowhere.'

Reinhardt gave a surly grunt. 'You would like to think so, wifey, but the truth will out one day.'

'But had he been strangled or what?' Irmelin asked.

'We don't know,' Kristine whispered.

'Did you try to find a pulse?'

'No,' Reinhardt said. 'There was no need for all that. His skin was turning blue, you know, marbled. I could tell instantly that he was dead.'

'Please can we change the subject?' Kristine pleaded.

Reinhardt looked at her across the table. 'It's actually very important to get these things out into the open,' he said. 'It's important to talk about them to get them out of your system.'

'But you don't want them out of your system.'

Reinhardt tossed his head. 'Listen,' he said sternly, 'I can talk about whatever I like. Do you have a problem with that?'

Irmelin and Kjell exchanged glances and Kristine fell silent. Then she got up and went out into the kitchen to make coffee. Irmelin followed her.

'I can't bear to hear him go on about it any longer, I'm trying to forget,' she whispered. She was making filter coffee, but had forgotten to count the measures of ground coffee. Irmelin looked at her with compassion; she, too, was appalled at the murder. This was not merely something they had read about in the paper, this was real to them.

'Do you know what he did?' Kristine whispered.

51

'He took pictures up there with his mobile.'

'What?' Irmelin's jaw dropped.

'He squatted down and took a load of pictures.'

'Not of the boy, surely?'

'Yes. And I bet he's showing them to Kjell.'

They listened towards the living room. The men had lowered their voices, but they could hear Kjell's deep bass and Reinhardt's tenor.

'I'm really scared he'll show them at work, too, that he'll sit in the canteen with his mobile showing them to all and sundry. You know what he's like.'

Irmelin fixed her with a stare.

'You never draw the line. You have to start putting your foot down, Kristine, he has far too much power over you.'

'I know.'

The coffee gurgled into the pot. Outside it was clouding over and the light in the kitchen grew dim.

'Everything's hopeless,' Kristine whispered. She shrugged forlornly. 'Some days I just want to pack my bags and leave. But I don't know where to go.'

'How long has this been going on?' Irmelin whispered back. 'It's been a long time since I last saw you looking really happy.'

Kristine thought about this.

'To tell you the truth, it's been going on for years. I can barely get through the days or the nights. Him lying next to me, breathing.'

She looked furtively at her friend, unsure how honest she should be. 'I don't even like the smell of him any more, I don't like his voice. He takes up so much space. I want him to sleep somewhere else. What I really want is to be on my own.'

'You're not frightened of him, are you?' Irmelin

said. 'That's not what we're talking about, is it?'

'No, I'm not scared of him. But when he goes on and on about something, it just wears me down.'

'You don't assert yourself.'

'I'm afraid to,' she said, ashamed. 'Because I don't know what's going to happen if I contradict him.'

Irmelin squeezed her hand.

'Try it once,' she said. 'Try it once and see what happens. He's not going to hit you, is he?'

'Oh, no, he would never hit me. But he breaks me in other ways. I'm such a coward.'

'You've got to stand up to him once and for all and tell him what you think,' Irmelin stated. 'He'll be able to handle it, you keep telling me how strong he is.'

'I'm scared that something will break,' she said, 'if I tell it like it is. If I start being completely honest with him, then nothing will be like it was before.'

'But you don't want it to be. Try something different, stand up for yourself and tell him what you think. Perhaps it'll turn out better than you imagine.'

Kristine fetched mugs from a cupboard and poured coffee.

'Most of all I want to leave,' she said, 'but I can't leave without taking something with me. If I don't have something to take with me, then all these years will have been for nothing.'

'Take something with you? What do you mean?'

'A child,' she said.

'But do you want a child with him? When you can't stand him?'

'Well, who else is there?' She shrugged

53

despondently. 'I'm thirty-seven years old.'

Then she pulled herself together and started to defend him.

'Perhaps he's just clueless,' she said. 'Perhaps he's as shocked as I am, and he can't think of any other way to express it. I mean, he's a man, after all. They're hopeless when it comes to showing their feelings.'

Irmelin shook her head. 'You always try to defend him,' she said. She got up and went over to the door to the living room; she hid behind it and spied on the men through the crack between the door and the frame.

'You were right,' she whispered. 'They're looking at the pictures now.'

CHAPTER 11

'Why are we so drawn to the death of others?' Skarre asked.

Sejer shook his head, he had never considered this question before. He was not drawn to death, he had never been seduced by sensation. Not even when he was a young officer.

'I'm not drawn to death,' he said. 'Are you?'

'But we chose this profession,' Skarre said. 'The murder of Jonas is a dreadful event. Others could have dealt with it, and we could be doing a much nicer job.'

Sejer started rolling a cigarette. He allowed himself one only every evening, as befits an exceedingly temperate man.

'A nicer job?' he asked suspiciously. 'Like what?'

'Well, you could have been a pastry chef,' Skarre suggested. 'You could have spent your whole day decorating cream cakes. And making tiny marzipan roses.'

'I could never have been a pastry chef,' Sejer declared. 'Cream cakes are pretty to look at, but they have no stories to tell. What would you have been doing?'

'I would have been a taxidermist.'

'Someone who stuffs dead animals, you mean?'

'Yes. Squirrels, minks and foxes.'

Sejer instinctively picked up his dog and put him on his lap. 'So tell me this,' he said. 'Why are you interested in criminals?'

'It's possible that somewhere deep inside I might be just a tad jealous of them,' Skarre said.

'Jealous? Of criminals?'

'They do what they want. They have no respect for authority: if they want something they just take it and they have nothing but contempt for us. It's a kind of protest, a deep and profound disdain. Personally, I am extremely law-abiding, to the point where it becomes scary, if you know what I mean. Why do you think people are so fascinated by crime?' he went on. 'Nothing sells better than murder and the worse it is, the more interested people are. What does that say about us?'

'I'm sure there are many answers to that,' Sejer said, 'and you're just as well placed to provide them as I am.'

'But you must have thought about it?'

'I think it has to do with the image we have of our enemy,' he said. 'All nations have an image of their enemy, you know, something that unites people. During the war we were united against the

55

Germans. It gave us a sense of identity and camaraderie, it made us take action and behave heroically. People were forced to choose sides, and in that way we could tell the good from the bad. But in our wealthy western world where peace and democracy reign, criminals have taken over this role. Their misdeeds unite us, we enjoy plenty of peace and quiet, but we also need excitement and stimulation to make us feel alive. But it's more than that. Every time someone's killed, we experience a kind of fortuitous assurance.'

'Why?' Skarre asked.

'It's the satisfaction of knowing that it wasn't you who committed this awful deed, because you're a good person; and you weren't the victim, either, because you're lucky, too. And then there's a third, uncomfortable, factor: some criminals acquire a heroic status. It might have to do with what you just said. Their lack of respect for the law and the authorities. We're terribly law-abiding individuals, but this slavish obedience in every aspect of our lives can lead to self-loathing.'

He looked over at Skarre.

'Would you do something for me, please?'

'Sure.'

'Would you go to that bookcase and get the first volume of the encyclopaedia?'

Skarre did as he was asked, he pulled out the heavy volume and placed it on Sejer's desk. Sejer eased the dog on to the floor, opened the book at 'A'. Skarre peered over his shoulder as he thumbed through the book.

'What are you looking for?'

Sejer glanced up at him. 'We're looking for a man.'

'Correct.'

'A killer,' Sejer added.

Skarre watched as he leafed through the book.

'And you think he's in the encyclopaedia? That would be a first,' he said.

Sejer continued for a while before finally stopping at a black and white portrait the size of a postage stamp.

'Hans Christian Andersen,' Skarre said.

They studied the picture in silence. Sejer noted the low, sloping forehead, the large nose, the high cheekbones and the crescent of curly hair at the back of his head. Precisely like Kristine Ris's description of the man by the barrier.

'How much do we see in a split second?' Sejer wondered. 'When we pass someone on the road?'

Skarre considered this. 'Not many details,' he stated. 'We see the sum total. And our brain will automatically look for a pre-existing, recognisable match.'

'Like the Danish writer.' Sejer said. 'His face is unique, don't you think? It's sensitive and strong at the same time.'

'He's not an attractive man,' Skarre declared.

'No,' Sejer said, 'there's a quality of weakness about him. And perhaps we'll lose our potential suspect tomorrow. Perhaps he'll come forward and prove to be completely innocent and we're back to square one. Perhaps he went for a walk, like people do on a Sunday in September.'

'Yes,' Skarre nodded. 'You might well be right.'

'Nevertheless,' Sejer went on, 'Reinhardt and Kristine Ris told us that he walked with a certain degree of difficulty. And if he finds it difficult to walk, he's unlikely to walk in the forest for pleasure. Unless he had to, because there was something he had to get rid of.'

Skarre nodded.

'Yet,' Sejer continued, 'doing what I'm doing now is risky.'

'What are you doing?' Skarre wanted to know.

'Fixating on him. Now all I see is the Danish writer. It blinds me to other things.'

'We found a small piece,' Skarre said, 'which might not even be part of the puzzle. It's always like this at the start of an investigation.'

'But this time we haven't got a minute to lose,' Sejer said, 'because this man will strike again.'

CHAPTER 12

He sat on his sofa, curled up in a corner.

He had turned off nearly all the lights and drawn the curtains. He liked the semi-darkness, it gave him a feeling of safety. In his hands he held the red Bermuda shorts. They were made from a fine, thin material, with white inner briefs and a small pocket. In the pocket he had found a sweet-smelling chewing gum wrapper. His first impulse, after what he preferred to call the 'accident', had been to burn the shorts in the stove. But he could not bear it, they belonged to him now, they would always belong to him. When he held them against his face he could detect a faint smell of urine, which he inhaled in deep breaths. He had sat like this for an eternity, while the hours slowly passed, while the light faded, only for a new day to dawn.

From now on nothing was safe. He could not be

certain of what the future held, if he even had a future, or if this was the end, the end of everything. He was incapable of eating anything and he had a splitting headache, it felt like knitting needles were piercing his temples. The telephone had rung, his father probably, but he had not answered it. He knew he ought to move to his bed, but he did not have the energy to get up, why should he get up? To make sure he got a good night's sleep? For the job he did not have? For people he did not know? At midnight he gave in, he lay down on the sofa on his side, still with the red shorts pressed against his face. At the end of the sofa lay an old woollen blanket. He got hold of it and covered his legs. He heard the ticking of the wall clock; it seemed louder than usual, as if every second warned of the impending disaster, the exposure and the condemnation, the verdict and the hatred, there were so many things. He felt dizzy. He visualised himself in court before a sea of hate-filled faces, they screamed at him, they spat and raged, they blamed him for everything, even his very existence, for who he was and what he had done. Meanwhile, he was shaking, trying to prepare an answer, but no sound came out, he had lost the power of speech. The images upset him. His pulse rose as if he had been running, though he had not moved for several hours.

When he finally slipped into a restless slumber, the memories racing past vividly brought it all back to him. The longing and the need he had lived with his entire life. The whole time, right up until this time, he had been able to control himself, he had turned away from every temptation. He had been strong and decent. But now fate had pushed him over the edge. He closed his eyes and a few dry sobs escaped, but they offered him no comfort.

CHAPTER 13

Inspector Sejer was always correct, reserved and polite. His formality might at times be mistaken for arrogance, unless you knew him well. Hardly anyone knew him well. He was totally devoted to his job, ambitious, but not a climber. He was patient, he listened, he had gravity and he hardly ever laughed. He took everything very seriously, life as well as his work, but on rare occasions his deep laughter could be heard. He was temperate, strong and decisive. He was always appropriately dressed, his shoes newly polished and in good condition, and his shirts freshly ironed. No one had ever taught him the art of flirtation, seduction or manipulation, unless he was facing a killer who denied all responsibility. Then he could charm the birds off the trees.

'Do you remember Jørgen Pihl?' Skarre asked. 'It was a fairly big case. He was a paediatrician at Ullevål Hospital, he treated kids the whole day and he had as much access to them as he could wish for. He finally went too far, the kids started talking. He was struck off, of course, and he went downhill from there, he started drinking, lost his home and his family.'

'Yes,' Sejer said, 'I remember him, and I remember Kristian Kruse. He held confirmation courses for the Humanist Society. And I remember Philip Åkeson.'

60

'No one will ever forget Philip Åkeson,' Skarre said. 'The man from Linde Forest hasn't contacted us,' he added. 'When do we start getting suspicious?'

'I already am,' Sejer said, 'but we should probably give him a few more days. There are people who don't follow the news.'

'I don't buy that,' Skarre said. 'This case has reached millions of people, it's gone beyond Norway, as has our request for him to get in touch. I'll give him until the end of the day and then I'll start suspecting him. Do we know anyone who walks with a limp?'

Sejer pondered this. 'No, I don't think so. But it might be an injury he's acquired recently.'

He went over to the window and looked out.'No matter who he is,' he said, 'whether he's got a record or not, he's gone underground. He's afraid to answer the telephone. He might wear different clothes, he might start to shop at a different supermarket. Whatever strength he's got left, he's using to build a defence for himself. He feels that the world is against him and he is most likely resentful.'

He looked at Jacob Skarre. 'Criminals have a peculiar view of themselves,' he said. 'They regard themselves as unique, exceptional even. They think they are smarter than most people. They think they can jump the queue and help themselves, the rules don't apply to them. If anyone gets hurt, they've only got themselves to blame. So if you want to rehabilitate an offender, in other words, you have to change his entire mindset and that's not easy. When it comes to our man, he might very well have a previous conviction, and if he has, he's

61

already an outcast. Once he's crossed the line he becomes even more dangerous; he has nothing to lose now. And if he's managed to suppress his paedophile tendencies for a long time, it might become harder for him now.'

'How do people develop such a predilection?' Skarre wondered. 'I don't understand it, it goes against nature. Kids don't send out sexual vibes.'

'That's what we need to find out,' Sejer said, 'and in order to do so we may have to put aside a great many prejudices.'

'That won't be easy,' Skarre said, 'I admit I have a lot of them.'

He leaned against the wall.

'A paedophile is someone who wanders around in shorts and a garish shirt on a beach in Thailand, watching kids play. He looks a bit scruffy. His pockets are stuffed with banknotes and he stays in a grotty room in a filthy hotel and he spends his evening in a bar. He watches people go by, while he drinks himself into a stupor. He drives a battered, old car filled with rubbish, newspapers and beer cans. Right, over to you.'

'He's weak, unsympathetic and self-obsessed,' Sejer said, 'with no friends, he's introverted and has some feminine features. His language is simple, he struggles to express himself. His mother was, or is, a domineering woman and he has never had the courage to stand up to her. His father was insignificant. He's an only child, anti-social and unattractive, he has little in the way of education and he's on a low income or on benefits. But when he's with kids he's in his element. Warm, approachable and friendly. Then he lights up and can do anything, he invites trust. What would you

62

have done,' he wondered, 'if you were nearly eight years old walking alone down the road? And a car pulled over and someone spoke to you?'

'I would have been scared,' Skarre said: 'scared that I had done something wrong and was about to be punished.'

'Punished? Why would you think that?'

'My father was a clergyman.'

*   *   *

Their intention was to drive to Huseby and retrace the route that Jonas August had taken on 4 September. According to Elfrid Løwe, this was a walk of around 1.8 kilometres, with scattered houses, a few farms and little traffic. They found the house where Jonas had been for his sleepover. His friend, Anders Wessel, stood in the open doorway with his mother; they both looked weighed down with guilt. Sejer and Skarre exchanged a few words with them and walked on. A group of kids of varying ages had spotted the police car and came running. Sejer thought back to his own childhood when a police car was enough to bring excitement to an otherwise dull day. It struck him how vulnerable they all were, you could easily tuck one under your arm and run off with them; they stood no chance when faced with an adult.

A little boy had summoned up the courage to come forward.

'Are you coming to get someone?'

'No,' Sejer said, 'we're looking for something.'

'What are you looking for?'

'We don't know,' Sejer said, 'but we think that if we look hard, we might find it.'

The boy accepted this explanation.

'Did you know Jonas August? He's got a friend here, and he visits him sometimes.'

The boy spoke again. 'Anders Wessel. He lives at number eight. His dad's Danish.' He turned around and pointed to the red house, which they had just visited. 'Jonas August is dead,' he added.

Sejer nodded gravely.

'We saw it on the telly,' the boy mumbled. 'There was a picture and everything. He was in Year Three. At Solberg School.'

The group was starting to get anxious.

'We think he might have got into a car,' Sejer said. 'When you're out walking you must always remember this: never accept a lift from a stranger. Has that ever happened to you? Has anyone ever stopped to offer you a lift?'

The children exchanged glances, as if they were having a silent conference. One of the boys thrust his fists into his pockets.

'There's a man who drives around here,' he said, 'and sometimes he rolls down his window and talks to us.'

This news made Sejer and Skarre exchange glances.

'What does he say to you?' Skarre asked.

'Nothing special. That my rucksack's great. Or that my trainers are cool. But they're not, they're hand-me-downs. Look, the sole's falling off.' He held out one foot to show them how worn his trainers were.

'Do you talk to him?' Skarre asked.

The boy dug the nose of his trainer into the sand.

'Don't talk to him,' Skarre said. 'Have you

64

mentioned this to your parents?'

His earnest tone made the boy anxious.

'No.'

'Why not?' Skarre asked him sternly.

'He hasn't done anything, he just drives around.'

Skarre quickly took his notepad from his inside pocket.

'His car,' he said. 'Can you describe it to us? Please, this is important.'

'Sure I can. It's a white car.'

'Big or small?'

'Not that small.'

'A saloon or a hatchback?'

He replied promptly and accurately. 'A saloon.'

Skarre looked up. He instantly recalled the description of the car that Mr and Mrs Ris had seen at Linde Forest.

'Has anyone else seen it?' he asked.

The kids nodded gravely.

'Sometimes he waits outside the school. And at the end of school, as soon as the bell goes, he starts driving slowly along the kerb.'

'Do you all go to Solberg School?'

'Yes,' a girl replied. 'But my friend goes to school in Midtbygda and she's seen him as well because he's everywhere.'

Sejer called them to attention. 'Listen to me,' he said. 'I want you to stay away from this man. Never accept a lift from him or get into his car, no matter what he says to you. Not all grown-ups are safe. Do you understand?'

Their small heads nodded.

'If he turns up again, I want you to go and find a grown-up straight away.'

The kids nodded once more. But then they

started giggling. The grown-ups had become so serious, and there were so many warnings to remember. They needed some comic relief. A girl held up her hand.

'He's got crooked teeth,' she said. 'They are on top of each other.' She pointed to her mouth with a dirty finger.

'His hair,' Sejer asked. 'What's his hair like?'

'It's grey. And a bit long.'

Sejer gave Skarre a job to do. 'I want you to call Solberg School. Speak to the head teacher. Tell the school to put someone on guard at the gates when they let the children out and to take down the registration number of that car if it turns up again. Also, they should send a letter to all parents recommending that those who can, collect their children rather than let them make their own way home.'

Skarre called directory enquiries to get the number.

Sejer looked back at the kids. 'Did that make you feel frightened?'

'Yes,' they whispered.

'Good,' Sejer said. 'That was my intention.'

CHAPTER 14

A charming farm lay at the foot of Solberg Hill.

The farmhouse was grey with two smaller wings, which enclosed the yard in a horseshoe shape. A framed wooden sign hung above the drive and announced that the name of the farm was 'Eikerhall'.

They crossed the yard.

'Farmers have so many things,' Skarre said. 'A huge house with lots of rooms. Storehouses and barns, horses and cattle, threshers and tractors, fields and meadows, while most people have sixty square metres in the city. If they're lucky they might have a balcony with a single potted plant and a cat that pees in a litter tray in the kitchen.'

Sejer looked at the farm: it was pretty and very well maintained, the lawns were green and lush.

'All the same I don't envy farmers,' Skarre continued. 'Well, not the ones who keep animals. They have to get up early every morning and they never get a day off. The cows are calving and the calf might get stuck or they get foot and mouth disease or they crash through the fence and wander into the road and some motorist ends up swerving into a ditch. Their days are filled with worries.'

'There's no limit to what you know about farmers,' Sejer commented.

He walked up to the front door. There was no doorbell; instead there was a large old-fashioned door knocker, a lion's head with a ring through its jaws. A woman appeared.

'Hello, we're retracing the walk Jonas August took on the fourth of September,' Sejer said, 'and yours is the first house on that route.'

She looked at them and nodded.

'Jonas passed your farm,' Sejer said, 'and then continued along Granatveien. Did you see him?'

'No,' she said. 'I didn't see him or anyone else. I don't know who he was, either, but my children go to Solberg School and they knew him. It's so awful I can hardly believe it,' she shuddered. 'Imagine there's a man like that in Huseby. I hope he's not from around here.'

'We got chatting to a group of children,' Sejer said. 'They mentioned a man in a white car who sometimes waits around the school gates. He rolls down the window and tries to chat to them. Did you know about this?'

'No,' she said, alarmed. 'No, I had absolutely no idea.'

'We've been in contact with the school,' Sejer said, 'and they will take precautions. But if your children know anything, you must get in touch with us.'

'Should we be scared?' she asked.

'Just take care,' Sejer said.

The two men walked on in silence. Occasionally a car or a tractor would pass them, but they were few and far between. After a while they came to a house on the right hand side of the road. An elderly man came out. He was tall and slim with grey hair, like Sejer.

'You're here about the boy?'

They nodded.

He showed them into the hall and walked over to the foot of the stairs where he called out for his wife, whose name was Gudrun. She appeared at the top of the stairs.

'I've already called you,' was the first thing she said. She walked down the stairs. 'Because I did see him. He walked right past our house, I've seen him many times.'

'And what was he wearing?'

'Like it said in the paper. Red shorts and a T-shirt.'

'Were you outside?' Skarre asked. 'Or did you

68

see him through the window?'

'I was standing on the veranda on the first floor shaking the duvets. He had a bat in his hand. Or rather, a long stick which he was swinging backwards and forwards.'

'Did he see you?' Skarre asked.

'He heard the sound of the duvets being shaken and he looked up.'

'How long were you out on the veranda?'

'Just a few minutes.'

'What about traffic?' Sejer asked. 'Did you see any cars once Jonas had passed?'

'I don't know much about cars,' she said apologetically. 'A car is just a car to me and there aren't many of them in Huseby. I've racked my brains, but I don't have anything else to tell you.'

'What time was it when the boy walked by?' Sejer asked.

'I'm sorry, I don't know. I don't wear a watch, you see.'

They thanked her and walked on. Soon the forest enveloped them, and they saw no houses, only dense, dark green spruces. After fifteen minutes they saw an attractive-looking farmhouse on the left hand side and further up to the right a small red cottage.

'You'll take the farmhouse,' Sejer said, 'and I'll take the cottage.'

Skarre crossed over to the farm while Sejer walked up to the cottage on the right. It was set back from the road and he doubted that the inhabitants would have had a view of Jonas August at all, even if he had got this far on his walk home. On the drive stood an old cart full of withered flowers. He found the doorbell and soon

69

afterwards a girl peered cautiously at him through a small crack in the door.

'Police,' he said bowing to her. 'Is there a grown-up at home?'

She looked about twelve; she wore glasses with steel frames, the sun was reflected in them.

'No,' she said, leaning against the door frame. 'They're at work.'

Sejer nodded in the direction of the road.

'I'm here about Jonas August,' he said. 'He walked along this road on Sunday the fourth of September. And I'm trying to find out if anyone in this house might have seen him. You've probably heard what happened.'

'We weren't at home at the time,' she said.

'Did you know him?'

'No,' she said, 'not really, but I know who he is.'

'You're at Solberg School, too?'

'Yes. I'm a Year Six.'

'I have another question for you,' Sejer said. 'Some children around here have told me about a man who sometimes waits outside the school when the bell goes in the afternoon. He drives a white car. Have you seen him?'

She shook her head. 'No, but I've heard about him. I've heard that he drives slowly up and down the road.'

Sejer looked at her closely. 'Why haven't you told a grown-up?'

She shrugged her slight shoulders.

'Not much to tell, really,' she said. 'He doesn't do anything, he just drives around.'

'Stay away from him,' Sejer ordered her.

She nodded.

'I'm sorry for disturbing you,' Sejer said. 'Are

you doing your homework?'

'I'm writing about Beethoven,' she said. 'He's our special topic.'

'He went deaf,' Sejer said, 'but you probably already know that.'

'Yes.'

'I've read that he was very difficult,' Sejer continued, 'a bitter old man who had gone deaf.'

The girl started to soften; a smile appeared on her face.

'But deaf or not,' Sejer went on, 'his head was full of music and there is something called the inner ear. And that's why he could write sonatas even though he had gone deaf. Quite impressive, don't you think?'

She nodded.

Sejer walked back down to the road as Skarre emerged from the farm shaking his head.

'Nothing.'

They were standing at the top of a steep hill. It plunged and disappeared into a bend, the forest grew denser and loomed like a wall on either side. Down in the valley they could hear the sound of running water. It was dark there. The road was fairly narrow, it started to disappear into the valley and at the bottom it made a sudden turn before it rose again up towards another hill. They stopped when they had reached the lowest point and looked at one another; they listened to the water roaring across the stones. Sejer took a few steps, then he paused and looked around.

'This is it,' he said, 'this is where it happened. At the foot of this hill. This is where he pulled over and took the boy.'

He bent down to pick something up.

71

'There's Jonas August's stick,' he said, 'the handle of an old shovel.'

CHAPTER 15

They searched the road and the verges, but found nothing else.

His mother's warnings had been brushed aside, barely noticeable, like the trace of a feather across a cheek and Jonas had discarded his stick and got into a stranger's car. People are unpredictable creatures, they invent rules which they break incessantly and they follow impulses which they later cannot explain.

Sejer and Skarre returned to their car. Spurred on by genuine curiosity and without any ulterior motives, they headed for the town and the older development by the river bank. One of the houses, a former pharmacy, was now the home of a convicted sex offender. His name was Philip Åkeson. They remembered him as mild and agreeable, open and generous by nature, and they decided to pay him a visit. It was unlikely to cause problems. During his trial eight years earlier, when he was charged with having indecently assaulted a number of young boys, he had charmed the whole courtroom by confessing to his passion for children with great enthusiasm and making no excuses of any kind. But also by making manifest to the jury the problem he represented. He never tried to justify himself or trivialise the assaults, he co-operated fully with the judicial system and confessed to everything. He wanted help and he was concerned about the boys he had abused. His plea was long and heartfelt, his tone was genuinely remorseful and on a few occasions he had displayed an infectious sense of humour. The words had flowed in a steady, mellifluous stream.

The men drove through the town with the river to their left, broad and swift.

'Well,' Skarre said in a somewhat patronising tone of voice, 'I know that paedophiles are human beings, too, even though they prefer kids. But it's difficult not to be repulsed by the mental images. It's hard to stay objective.'

'It is,' Sejer agreed, 'but we have to. It's one thing to have fantasies, quite another to carry them out. My guess is that the number of actual paedophiles is high and that's worrying. They have to hide away the whole time, they always have to pretend.'

'Why are they mainly men?' Skarre wondered.

'Well,' Sejer said, 'I'm no expert, but women are much better at intimacy and emotions than men. What we're dealing with here are men who aren't in touch with their own feelings. They need an object in order to connect to their feelings. They try to solve the problem by developing paraphilia. Paraphilia means "to love something else".'

He stopped at a red light. 'I mean, something outside the norm. Some desire very young children, others want them as they reach puberty. Some fall deeply in love with a specific child and others are attracted to children in general because they are small and fragile, and because they can be controlled.'

The light changed to green; he drove on. 'It's actually interesting,' he said. 'Whereas gay men

73

have finally become accepted, paedophiles will forever be outcast. They will remain the object of the utmost contempt, they will never be understood.'

He pulled in and parked outside the green pharmacy. Shortly afterwards they noticed the white curtain twitch.

Åkeson opened the door to them before they even had time to ring the bell. He had not changed. His face was remarkably round and smooth, his eyes brown and alert, they lit up at the sight of the two men. He had very little hair left, just a few tufts, which looked like white candyfloss; a few strands kept falling across his forehead. He had a round body with short limbs and now he held out a hand and greeted them effusively.

'Well, I never,' he said. 'So you two gentlemen have come out for a stroll. Of course, I have read quite a lot about you in the papers recently, this is a serious business, that much I have understood. I recognise you, Sejer. You still tower over the rest of us, if I may say so, but it's meant as a compliment. Whereas you,' he looked at Skarre, 'I do believe I've forgotten your name. Or, rather, I only remember your curls. Do the police really allow you to grow your hair that long? I thought uniform guidelines were much stricter than that. What is your name again?'

'Skarre,' said Skarre.

'Of course. So it is. Skarre. And you roll your r's because you're from the south, how very charming. But please, do come in, come in, come in. It was only a matter of time before you would come knocking on my door, I knew that, but I also know that you know that I'm not involved, so I'm

74

delighted to welcome you to my humble abode. Yes, truly delighted, I don't get many visitors. I do hope you're not in a hurry,' he said chattily, 'so we can have ourselves a nice long natter, I'd appreciate that, I really would.'

He padded into the house and showed them the way. His living room was cosy and a touch feminine with wall-to-wall carpet and wicker furniture. From the living room there was a view of the river and outside a few steps led into a small garden which ended right at the water's edge. A fat, sprawling cat was lazing about in an armchair on something that looked liked a goatskin. On the windowsills were flowering begonias, blossoming prodigiously.

Åkeson gestured towards the armchairs. 'Just chuck the cat aside,' he said speaking to Skarre. 'That cat is so lazy, I don't know what to do about him. Do you think he can be bothered to go hunting? Oh, no, he just lies there the whole day holding court. Can I tempt you with a cup of tea?'

He bustled around like an old woman.

'No, thank you, Åkeson,' Sejer said. 'Please sit down. You know we're very busy at the moment. And you already know why we're here. Or to put it another way, we don't have that many places to go.'

Åkeson let himself flop into the wicker armchair. He crossed his legs and folded his hands across his knee.

'True, and I have to say this,' he said. 'You've got to catch this man. We can't have this, I'm sure you'll agree.'

'We agree,' Sejer said kindly. His eyes rested on Åkeson's face and the sight of it made him smile.

Skarre shifted the cat on to the floor and sat

75

down on the goatskin.

'He might strike again.' Åkeson said. 'I hope to God not, but that's how it is: once you've crossed that line, it's easy to keep going.'

'So you know something about this?' Skarre asked cautiously.

'I see things on the television,' Åkeson said, 'and I've been thinking that he might be a first timer.'

Sejer pricked up his ears. 'What makes you think that?'

'Well, he's kept a lid on things, a whole lifetime perhaps, possibly by being married. I'm only guessing here. His marriage breaks down and he's all alone in the world. He might have children of his own, but he no longer has any contact with them. The pressure grows until finally he snaps and when he comes to his senses again, he panics.'

Åkeson looked at them with his brown eyes.

'I mean,' he said theatrically, 'we need to ask ourselves the following question: are we looking for an experienced, predatory paedophile? Has this man invited boys to his house for years, has he been befriending them, giving them money, grooming them? And if so, why did it suddenly go wrong?'

Sejer and Skarre looked at each other.

'Are you sure you don't want a cup of tea after all?' Åkeson asked. 'I've got some custard creams. If you fancy some.'

'You're very kind,' Sejer said, 'but we're on duty and we can't stay for long.'

'Then I won't ask you again,' he said, 'though the golden rule for being a good host is to always ask three times. Anyway, you need to understand this man and what kind of preferences he has. Is he

76

looking for any kid, or just boys, and in that case what type of boy? I mean, we're as discerning as anyone else, we don't swoon at just anyone coming our way.'

'Are you in touch with other paedophiles, Åkeson?' Skarre asked.

'Every now and then.'

'Have you noticed anyone in particular? Is there anyone who stands out?'

'No, not really. And there's not always much support to be had there, either, it depends on the individual. You know me, of course, and you know that I'm a simple soul who keeps myself to myself. So despite the tragic circumstances, I'm awfully pleased that you came to see me.'

Skarre struggled to suppress a smile; it was impossible not to be charmed by this short, gentle man.

'Jonas August came from Huseby,' Sejer said. 'He lived on Granatveien. And he went to Solberg School, he was in Year Three. Do you know a man who drives around in his car watching the children when they make their way home from school? A white car?'

Åkeson frowned. 'No, I don't know anyone like that. Rather risky, I would have thought. Personally I go into town. I sit on a bench in the centre and watch the kids, but I never touch them. You can always dream. My thoughts are free!' He erupted into a big smile.

Sejer and Skarre forced themselves not to laugh.

'So you stay away from schools?' Sejer asked.

'I don't draw attention to myself, is how I'd put it.'

Sejer had got up and was now studying a

77

photograph on the wall. A black boy with dark eyes and bright white teeth.

'Isn't he gorgeous?' Åkeson said. 'I found him in a Red Cross calendar. I had to have him on my wall, I'm allowed that. But let me add that if I had been in Nigeria and actually met the poor lad, I would have given him something to eat first. I mean before I did anything else.'

'You've had therapy, haven't you, Åkeson?' Skarre asked.

'Indeed I have. I saw a psychosexual counsellor for quite a while.'

'Did it help you?'

'Of course it did. I finally got a chance to talk about how I feel, to explain myself. Not many people are prepared to listen to us, or treat us with respect. You two are a rare exception, believe you me.'

'Can I ask you a very personal question?' Skarre asked.

Åkeson leaned forward. 'Of course you can, young man, fire away. I'm no weakling, I just look like one.'

'Have you ever had a relationship with an adult woman?'

Åkeson smiled coquettishly. 'Well,' he said, pausing theatrically as was his style, 'that depends how you define adult. Yes, of course I have. But I must add that she was a terribly delicate little thing. It didn't last very long, I think it was mainly a desperate attempt to be normal; there's nothing we would rather be, we would prefer to be like you. But, dear Lord, I'm a grown man, I turned fifty last year and I know who I am, it can't be denied and I don't want to either. And that poor little boy up in

78

Linde Forest, words cannot express how I feel. I lay awake half the night, I just couldn't take it in. He was strangled, I suppose? I mean, I'm thinking about his mother and everything she has to go through. Just so you know, none of us feels good about this.'

'We believe you,' Sejer said. 'And we won't take up any more of your time.'

'But don't you want to know where I was on the fourth?' Åkeson asked innocently; he was trying to make the two men stay for as long as possible.

'Certainly,' Sejer said benevolently. 'Where were you on the fourth, in the afternoon?'

'I went to an antiques fair in the town hall,' Åkeson said eagerly. 'It's an annual event, first weekend of September. I normally go, you can find all sorts of hidden treasures and I'm usually lucky.'

'Are you?' Sejer said patiently.

'I bought teacups,' he said happily. 'I bought four and they are truly amazing. French Garden from Villeroy and Boch. They cost me eight hundred kroner. Let me add that if I had bought them in Glassmagasinet, they would have cost me fourteen hundred. And I haven't even had an opportunity to show them to you; that was the reason I wanted to make you tea. I've got the receipt somewhere, and the lady who sold them to me would remember me, I just know she would. I don't blend in. I know I'll get noticed, but I can't be bothered to be ashamed of it.' He brushed a few strands of hair aside. All the time smiling his gleaming smile and displaying his alert nature.

Then he escorted them out. He patted Skarre on the shoulder and detained them with small talk for as long as he could.

'Goodness gracious, how stimulating it is to have company,' he said.

'If you hear any rumours,' Sejer said, 'you'll call us, won't you?'

'That goes without saying; I'll run to the telephone. But there won't be any rumours. Your man won't surface for a long time.'

CHAPTER 16

He had been sleeping with the red shorts pressed against his face. Now he realised that their smell, this tantalising, acidic smell, a mixture of seawater and sweet apples, was slowly starting to fade. He pressed them hard against his nose, his eyelids closing once again. For a long time he lay like this feeling grief and loss, a weight that dragged him deep into the mattress. The sun crept in through a gap between the curtains, it warmed his skin. His eyes were beginning to sting. He thought about the boy he had carried through the forest. There was not an ounce of fat on his slender body, only flesh and bones, only blue veins and tiny, marbled nails. He fantasised about how appetising the little boy had been, his fingers, his earlobes, his toes. He forced his thoughts away, they terrified him, they were delicious, forbidden and secret.

He got up and went into the kitchen and peered inside the fridge. There was hardly any food, he had not been shopping for ages. All he found was some ham with its edges curled up and a tub of rancid butter. The bread had gone stale and was covered by a layer of blue-green mould. But he had a litre of fresh milk and a jar of raspberry jam. He mixed some milk and jam in a old jam jar, and tightened the lid before shaking it. When it was well blended and the milk had turned pink, he drank it straight from the jar; it tasted good. For a while he leaned against the counter, feeling how the sweetened drink gave him strength.

He knew that the red shorts had to go. He had disposed of the trainers by dumping them in a clothes collection point in the town centre. If the police arrived, they were bound to turn over the house, he knew he would have to be prepared for that, but he could not bear to part with the red shorts. Resolutely he went into his bedroom to fetch the shorts. He rolled them into a tight sausage and hid them at the bottom of a box of cornflakes which he placed at the far end of the cupboard. He felt he had been very clever. They'll never think to look there, he thought. At night, he would get out the shorts and take them with him to bed. Because they would never turn up at night, he was convinced of that, the nights were his own, the few free ones he had left.

He went over to the window. He parted the curtains slightly and looked out at the farmhouse, at the red barn. A blue tractor was parked in the farmyard, where there was a maple tree with a large, lush crown. He had rented the cottage for years, it was over a hundred years old and in very bad condition. The bedroom walls were covered by slimy mould. He had heard that mould released a gas which could be toxic. Not that he cared about that, his life was not worth a great deal, he was certainly not clinging to it. The house did not have a bathroom either, just an old shower cubicle in a

81

corner of the kitchen with a tatty, yellow shower curtain covered with mildew. Nevertheless the cottage had a certain appeal; it had a history and charm. Little, square windows with broad windowsills and thick beams in the ceiling. Hops grew around the entrance. The cottage was situated in a dip and the big, white-painted farmhouse towered at the top of the hill. The farmer lived there with his wife and four daughters. Every summer the girls would lie on the lawn in tiny bikinis, lined up like a row of golden fish fillets. He never even so much as looked at them. Adjacent to the farmhouse was another cottage where the farmer's mother lived; she was eighty-six.

Four Polish men would turn up to work in the fields every May and they would stay on until November. They were nodding acquaintances, but he never stopped to talk to them. They slept in the storehouse. Sometimes, in the evenings, he would hear laughter and voices coming from in there, in a language he did not understand but found exotic. One of them was good at playing the mouth organ and another had a distinctive laugh, which would roll across the farmyard from time to time. They were polite, friendly and hard-working people.

As he stood there staring out into the farmyard it suddenly occurred to him that pulling the curtain had been a stupid thing to do. He was not in the habit of doing that and it might arouse suspicion. He flung the fabric aside and the light flooded in. Whether he wanted to or not, he would have to start his car and go food shopping. His white car. The car they were looking for. And he would buy a newspaper, obviously, if he could muster the courage. How much did they know, what had they found, were they about to catch him, was it only a matter of days before they would break down his door? He remembered his anorak, he could never wear it again, he had to get rid of it. He hurried out into the hall to see what else was hanging on the coat stand. A coat with big pockets and an old leather jacket, its lining had practically been worn away and the leather had cracked on the elbows. In the pocket he found an ancient cinema ticket and the stick from an ice-cream.

He went back into the kitchen to have a shower, pulled aside the shower curtain, stepped inside and turned on the taps. While he showered he made more plans. Don't change your habits, he thought, keep doing the things you always did, say hello to people and be friendly, or better still, fling out your arms and laugh heartily. Go outside and wash the car, perhaps, give the Poles a friendly nod, talk about the weather. If anyone heard a rumour about him, they would dismiss it instantly. Not him, they would say, he's behaving completely normally.

CHAPTER 17

Isn't it odd, Kristine mused, that I can be absolutely certain that Reinhardt has come home, when I haven't even seen him yet. Everyone has their own individual sound, their particular way of going through the rooms. Reinhardt was a big man; he was not in the habit of tiptoeing around the place. A hanger clattered on to the floor, she heard the thud as he kicked off his shoes, first one then the other.

'Hello, sweetheart!'

He had a thick bundle of newspapers tucked under his arm. Kristine appeared from the kitchen.

'How long are you going to keep buying all those papers?'

'As long as there's something about Jonas Løwe,' he said. 'Look, plenty of coverage.'

He held up *Dagbladet* to show her.

'There's a photo of Jonas on the front page again today, it's a unique case in Norwegian crime history, do you realise that? I want to know all about it, every detail.'

He gestured towards the growing pile of old newspapers. 'You're always telling me to get a hobby, that I should be doing something other than playing computer games. I've come to a decision. I will follow this case every day until it has been solved and when they get him, I'll follow his trial.'

Kristine snatched *Dagbladet* from his hands. She leafed through it, scanning it quickly.

'But there's nothing new,' she said. 'They just repeat the same old stories.'

'Don't throw them away,' he said. 'I need to cut out the articles.'

'What do you mean, cut them out?'She gave him a puzzled look.

'As a matter of fact,' he said solemnly, 'it's terribly interesting, for once, to follow a case right from the start, follow it week by week as it develops. It's like a discipline of some sort.' He ran his fingers through his hair. 'Perhaps I should quit my job at Hafslund and become a crime reporter. I think I've got the bug.'

84

Kristine shook her head in disbelief.

'When I think about it,' he reasoned, 'I realise that I have never read the news in this way before. I've been superficial. None of the world's misery has ever gripped me. But this has, it's a totally new sensation.'

He let himself flop into a chair and grabbed hold of *VG* magazine.

'But why?' she asked.

'Because we found him, Kristine. It's that simple.'

'But we didn't know him.'

'I feel I know him now. I've been reading about Jonas for days. The whole sequence of events rolls before my eyes like a film.'

'But we don't know the sequence of events,' she reminded him. 'Look here.'

She pointed and read aloud: ' "The police have released very little information about Jonas August and his tragic death".'

'Well,' Reinhardt said, 'if you ask me I would say that means they've no idea what happened, but they're afraid to admit it, they don't want to lose face.'

Kristine continued to look at him sceptically.

'We saw him, Kristine,' Reinhardt went on. 'We saw him quite clearly. You and I are the only two people in the world to have seen him in person. In fact, I see him more clearly now than I did then. I'd recognise the bastard anywhere.'

'But we don't know if he really was the killer,' she said. 'You just can't say things like that. All he did was walk past us, and he was startled, but that's normal.'

Reinhardt thumbed through the newspaper.

'Take a look here, then, if you don't believe me. Listen to this: "After several days the mystery man from Linde Forest has yet to come forward." There. Now he's finally become the mystery man. But you and I knew that instantly.'

'Perhaps he's shy and introverted,' she said. 'Perhaps he's gone abroad.'

'The latter I can believe,' Reinhardt said. 'In which case he must be guilty. My theory is that this is a straightforward case: the man we met killed Jonas August. He walked right into us and he panicked. He has probably bought all the newspapers today as well, and right now he's going though them with his heart pounding.'

Kristine went back out into the kitchen. It disturbed her that he was so obsessed by the murder. Then she wondered if he would start looking for something else once the case had been solved or whether he would become his old self again. She did not want that either, she liked neither the new nor the old version of Reinhardt. And again she felt ashamed, as she always did. She felt the days had become so unreal, she felt the harvest sunlight was too harsh, the night air too raw, the wind too sharp. She thought Reinhardt was behaving strangely. She took out a packet of ox liver from the fridge and started trimming the dark pieces with a knife. Reinhardt came over to stand next to her and he patted her cheek affectionately.

'Now what's that serious face all about, wifey?' he joked.

She continued cutting without answering. The liver oozed blood, the chopping board grew wet and slippery.

86

'You're gripped by this too,' he claimed, 'but for some reason you won't admit it. You have your reasons, I suppose.'

She continued to stay silent.

'Everyone's talking about it,' he pressed on. 'People are interested in these things, of course they are.'

'But talking isn't enough for you,' she said. 'You wallow in it.'

'I cut interesting articles out of newspapers,' he said. 'Now don't exaggerate.'

Again she refused to reply.

Suddenly he changed the subject. 'Shall I tell you a secret?' he said. 'I've always hated liver.'

At this she looked up quickly. 'But you eat it. You always have.'

'Yes,' he said, placing his hands on her shoulders. 'Because you put it in a casserole. With onion, mushrooms and bacon. That makes even liver appetising.'

She kept working, her fingers moving swiftly. She hated him being so close to her, and it confused her when his moods changed so rapidly.

'Where do you think he lives, Kristine?' Reinhardt asked as he buried his face in her neck. 'I think he lives somewhere isolated. I can't imagine him right in the middle of some huge residential estate. Or perhaps he's got an old, ramshackle house his mother left him, something in the forest. Or an old, crumbling cottage.'

'We don't know the first thing about where he lives,' she said in an exasperated voice.

'No, I'm just speculating. That's what the police are doing when they have nothing else to go on. They know a lot about people who eat small children.'

'Eat them?' she shuddered.

'It's just an expression,' he smiled. 'Now, don't go getting all serious. But one thing's certain: Jonas August is becoming a celebrity. There's been plenty of interest from foreign papers, and he is unique in Norwegian crime history. They always take girls, you know. Women and girlfriends. Or ex-girlfriends. This is different. You don't understand,' he said abruptly. 'You don't understand how exceptional this is.'

Kristine cut the liver into thin strips.

'Yes,' she sighed, 'this is exceptional. It makes me dizzy,' she admitted.

'And we're a part of it,' he said.

'We're not.'

'You don't want to be,' he corrected her. 'That's a different matter. You just want to move on, you want to forget about it. You're a true woman, you shy away from confrontation.'

'Yes,' she said. 'I want to move on. You're utterly wrong. There is nothing we can do, Reinhardt, let the police deal with it, please!'

'Like I thought,' he said. 'You don't appreciate how serious this is. But you and I can identify him, we can place him at the crime scene, or a few metres away from it at any rate. Don't you understand how important we are? The police need us. Think about it: we can put him away for twenty-one years!'

He was becoming melodramatic, the pitch of his voice was rising. She turned on the cooker and put butter in the frying pan.

'I can barely recall what he looked like,' she said.

Reinhardt's jaw dropped. 'How can you say

that? You were so sure back then. About his clothes and everything? Hans Christian Andersen, that's what you said, wasn't it? Hans Christian Andersen, of all things.'

'Yes,' she said reluctantly, 'but I'm not so sure any more, about any of it.'

Reinhardt folded his arms across his chest. 'But I am. I'm sure. And there's nothing wrong with my eyesight.'

The butter was browning, she added the liver; the smell spread through the kitchen.

'There must have been something wrong with his parents,' Reinhardt said distantly.

She glanced at him across her shoulder.

'Why?'

'Since he turned into a pervert.'

'We can't be sure of that, can we?' she said. 'We don't know if it had anything to do with his parents.'

'People don't get damaged for no reason,' he said.

She added seasoning, inhaled the good smell.

'It's a case of being in the wrong place at the wrong time,' Reinhardt went on. He was leaning against the worktop and he shook his head sadly. 'I mean, poor little Jonas August, who came walking along the road on the very day, the very moment the killer drove past. What are the chances of that?'

Kristine turned over the liver in the frying pan. The strips were browning nicely.

'I really don't think this was premeditated,' she said. 'Perhaps he hadn't even planned it, perhaps he just passed him in his car and acted on impulse.'

'That's precisely what we're talking about,'

89

Reinhardt said. 'An inability to control impulses.'

'Have you deleted all those pictures?' she asked.

He tossed his head. 'Why do you keep going on about them?'

'Have you shown them to people at work?'

She moved the frying pan away from the heat.

'What if I have? I don't understand why you're getting so worked up about them, people are naturally curious.'

She turned away again before replying. 'They were never meant for public consumption,' she said.

'And who decided that?'

Suddenly she felt exhausted. She leaned against the cooker and felt the heat from the brown butter waft against her face.

'Common decency,' she whispered. 'Have you never heard of that?'

CHAPTER 18

He put on the old leather jacket. It was so worn he felt like a beggar, but he could not worry about that. His hair was unkempt, too, it was a long time since he had last had it cut. His benefits never stretched to haircuts, he always had to economise. He was forced to go out, he had to drive the white car through the streets because there was no food left in the house. He had starved these last few days, he was starting to waste away. The daylight terrified him, but he made himself leave the house. I'm still alive, he thought, I'm still free. At the last minute he fetched an old cap and put it on his head, pulled the brim down and went over to the mirror. He thought it was a good disguise. The car was only a few steps away. At this very moment the farmer's old mother came hobbling across the farmyard, her chin jutting out, her back hunched. She used to run this farm. In her day there had also been a herd of dairy cows here, now only the chickens were left and some black and white rabbits in a hutch behind the barn.

She spotted him and waved, but he swiftly opened the car door and got in. He did not want to talk, not to anyone. But she started shuffling at great speed. Something was clearly going on and his fear of seeming desperate made him wait. She leaned against the car and peered down at him with watery eyes. Reluctantly he rolled down the window.

'You're going into town, aren't you?'

He nodded. When women grow very old they seem to develop a sixth sense, he thought.

'Need to do a bit of shopping,' he said, forcing a weak smile. He had nothing against her, in fact he rather liked the grey, old woman. He could not imagine the farm without her, and he liked it when she pottered around with her hands folded behind her back.

'We all need to eat,' she said.

Her dress was faded and worn; he noticed that a few buttons were missing and he could see an old-fashioned pink slip with a narrow lace trim underneath it. Her hair was dry and white and stuck out from underneath a blue headscarf.

'Have you seen all those cars?' she asked. 'All those photographers and reporters? They've come to ask about the boy. The one they found up in

91

Linde Forest.'

'Yes,' he croaked. 'I've seen them.'

'Poor little lad.'

'Yes,' he said. 'It's awful.'

'Police cars too,' she added, 'all over the place. And it's been fifty years since the last time.'

'The last time since what?' he asked.

'Since anyone committed a murder here in Huseby.'

He gave her a confused look.

'Oh, you didn't know?'

'No,' he replied.

She swaggered a little because she had something to impart.

'The eldest son at Fagre Øst killed his sweetheart. She was only fifteen. Pregnant too, she was, that's how young people are, they sleep together and, of course, it has consequences. He was sent down for a very long time. He moved to the other end of the country when he got out, needless to say. He's on benefits now. I suppose he's sitting somewhere moping about what happened.'

He listened to her stream of words. He wondered if she wanted something from him or whether she was just in search of an audience.

'But to go for small children is absolutely unforgivable, in my opinion.'

She was fiddling with her headscarf with a wrinkled hand. Her nails were long and curved.

'Adults beating each other black and blue, that's one thing. But he was only a little lad.'

He nodded. She was not looking at him now, she was talking into the air while she clawed at the car door as if to stop him from leaving because she had so much to tell him.

'Anyway,' she said, 'there was something I wanted to ask you. It's only a small thing. If it's not too much trouble. I don't want to be a nuisance.' She scrutinised him with her faded blue eyes. 'But if you don't ask, you don't get, so the saying goes.'

He waited patiently. It was a question of giving her time. The very old, he thought, they trap us in their slowness, it's like being caught in a mass of seaweed. He looked into her withered face; her skin hung loose around her neck and some stray, straggly hairs protruded from her chin. She's no longer feminine, he thought, she's no longer attractive. She's alone at life's outpost and she's waiting. He wondered what it was like to go to bed at night when you were eighty-six, the feeling as the darkness crept out from every corner, perhaps it was the final darkness.

'The lads, you know,' she said nodding in the direction of the storehouse. 'The lads,' she said again, 'they've got nothing to do in the evenings, they miss their wives and their children. I rack my brains trying to think of something for them to do.'

She was referring to the Poles. She paused. She bent down to look at him as he sat there waiting, impatiently, with his hands on the wheel. It cost him a great deal to look her in the eye, she was so firm and staunch and decent that she glowed.

'They don't want to spend any money either, they never go out, they just sit there, bored. They play cards,' she explained: 'poker, I think. But they never play for money, they're so thrifty. We could learn something from them, we live to excess. Well, you might be an exception, I didn't mean it like that. What I was saying was, we're quite spoilt, you

93

can't deny that.'

He waited for her to tell him what she wanted. He was desperate to get away.

'No, what I wanted to ask you was this,' she continued: 'if you might have an old travel radio. The sort with an aerial and batteries, you know. There's no power in the storehouse. That would be a fine thing,' she added, 'if there was power in the storehouse. As if we haven't got enough expenses here on the farm as it is.' She laughed a creaking laughter. He failed to see what was so funny.

'I haven't had one of those for years,' he said, turning on the engine. 'I used to own an old Kurér, but I threw it away. Or perhaps I gave it to a charity,' he added.

He revved the engine. She moved, shaking her head. The knot of the headscarf at the back of her head reminded him of a bird with blue wings, it bobbed up and down when she moved.

'It would have been nice for them to have a bit of music,' she said. 'The evenings are so long. They're here from May to November, that's six months away from their families. Away from all the little things.' She fell silent once more, supporting herself on the car with a pale hand.

The whole country is out looking for me, he thought, and she's asking me if I have an old radio. He gripped the steering wheel tightly as a feeling of panic began to surge in him, a sense of violent, internal pressure because he was about to mix with other people and it terrified him.

'Never mind. I shan't keep you any longer,' she said. 'They'll probably manage without one. I'm just an old woman and I worry about these things. I don't have much else to do. And nobody cares about the things that I know and could tell them about, they want to find out everything for themselves. That's the way life goes, you're just told to shut up and go away, but I'm here now and I'm not going anywhere.'

She smiled and displayed a set of worn, yellow teeth before hobbling off again. He saw her hunched figure disappear towards the greenhouse. It had been years since it had last been in use, most of the windows were broken and weeds covered the frame vigorously like lianas in the jungle. And he thought that he was like the old greenhouse. The façade was worn and battered and inside forbidden urges ran riot.

Finally he was free to drive off. He stopped by his letter box and picked up a pile of junk mail, throwing everything on the floor of the car before turning out on to the main road. He started looking out for white cars. To his infinite delight he spotted them regularly, a Subaru, a Toyota Hiace, an Opel. While he drove, he remembered his mother and her many mood swings. I was a nervous child, he thought. My mother made sure of that. She was always ready with a threat, a telling-off, a cutting remark. I grew up in an ocean of reproaches.

His thoughts depressed him, and he felt his mood darken.

CHAPTER 19

'This reminds me of something,' Sejer said. 'Something from my childhood.'

'What is it?' Skarre asked.

He was sitting with Sejer's dog on his lap and playing with its velvety ears.

'I had a bicycle with a dynamo,' Sejer said, 'which would light up if I pedalled hard enough. At this point in the investigation, it's a question of keeping the speed going and then I will be able to understand what led to the death of Jonas August.'

'Is it necessary for you to understand?' Skarre asked. 'Isn't it enough to discover the truth?'

'No, it's not. The man who took Jonas's life needs to explain to me every single detail in the series of events which led to Jonas's death. He must give me a second by second account of why it had to end in tragedy.'

'Is that what we're dealing with here?' Skarre asked. 'A tragedy?'

'We might be.'

'So you equate solving a crime with reconciliation? And feel better about it?'

Sejer considered this. 'No, no, it's not about that. Only Elfrid has the right to forgive.'

'So why are you talking like this?' Skarre asked.

'Because I need reassurance,' he said, 'that pure evil is a rare event.'

'Is it?'

'I want it to be.' He looked at Skarre and nodded. 'Yes,' he said, 'it's rare.'

'Well,' Skarre said, 'this is really nothing like the

light on your bicycle. And you can't complain about the speed. Everyone is working overtime, every single day, or in other words, we're pedalling as if our lives depended on it.'

Sejer switched off his desk lamp. They had both been working for fourteen hours, it was time to go home, but they were reluctant. Leaving felt like letting Jonas August down.

'Why don't we go for a beer?' Skarre suggested.

Sejer weighed up the pros and cons. He was not the type to drink alcohol whenever the opportunity presented itself, he was not an impulsive man, but he agreed. They went out into the busy street, the dog half running alongside them to keep up. For a while they walked in silence, the older man and the younger, and as they approached a level crossing, they noticed two girls coming towards them. The girls walked closely together on the pavement and they walked arm in arm like girls do, their heels clicking against the tarmac like castanets.

'Take a look at those two,' Skarre said.

Sejer looked at the girls. They were smooth and firm like tulips right before they bloom. A low, intimate chatter flew through the September air.

'How old would you say they were?' Skarre asked.

Sejer studied the girls.

'Sixteen, perhaps?'

Skarre rolled his eyes. 'Honestly, you're miles off, they're thirteen or fourteen. Remember there's a lot of icing on those cakes.'

'Icing?'

'Make-up.'

They passed the girls. Skarre sent them one of his most dazzling smiles.

'Not a day over fourteen,' Skarre whispered.

'Where are you going with this?'

'I'm flying a kite; we work with morality and it gives rise to plenty of food for thought. Imagine a young man out looking for a girlfriend. My point is: the girls look like this and yet they're still off limits. And I'm thinking about the age of consent, it's sixteen in Norway.'

'Correct,' Sejer said. 'Do you have any objections?'

'Perhaps it should be lower,' Skarre. 'What kind of signals were they sending out, the two girls we just passed? Here we are, arm in arm, we're attractive and we're up for anything.'

Sejer turned to get a second look.

'If one of them meets a boy,' Skarre said, 'and they end up in bed and she later regrets it, he could be put away for two to three years. And labelled a sex offender.'

'We need to have some rules,' Sejer stated. 'We must protect children and we do that by setting a limit.'

'But girls today are so grown up,' Skarre said. 'And whether we like it or not, they're sexual beings.'

'You don't have children,' Sejer said, 'you don't understand the instinct to protect them. It rises up in you, once you're responsible for another human being. A young person,' he added, 'your beautiful daughter, perhaps, goes out into the world. Only you aren't allowed to come with her any more, you just have to stay at home and wait for her to come back. While you imagine the worst.'

*   *   *

98

They made themselves comfortable with their beers.

'The thing is,' Skarre said, 'I was wondering if we could have a chat about sex.'

Sejer bent down and started patting his dog. 'You go first,' he said quickly.

'In Sweden,' Skarre went on, 'the age of consent is fifteen.'

'Right.'

Sejer was drinking Pilsner Urquell. His face had a closed expression, but he was paying attention.

'In other words,' Skarre continued, 'a man is branded a sex offender and given a severe sentence in Norway, but the same act is legal in Sweden.'

'Is that a problem?'

'Of course it is, it's too arbitrary. The problem with sex is that it becomes about morality. Let's take another example,' he said. 'Think of oral sex.'

Sejer kept his eyes firmly on his dog.

'In a few states in the US it's considered a perversion,' Skarre said, 'and consequently it's a criminal offence. My point is: what's abnormal, what's perverted? And what constitutes an assault?'

'We're working in Norway,' Sejer said, 'and here the rules are clear. And we should be thankful for that.'

'Possibly,' Skarre said. 'But there's something else I've been thinking about quite a lot, there's something we have to face up to. When it comes to paedophiles, it's a fact that the offender himself has been unable to develop normally. He may himself have been the victim of abuse and he seeks out children to solve a problem. I just wanted to

99

remind you of that side of the argument.'

'Many people have problems,' Sejer said. 'There are several acceptable ways of solving them and then there are unacceptable ways. Many paedophiles never give in to their urges, it's a question of staying in control. Our man didn't do that.'

'Nevertheless,' Skarre said, 'the possibility that he was himself abused is high. Up to seventy per cent have been. Perhaps he should receive treatment rather than condemnation. Any lawyer who knows their stuff would exploit this for all it's worth.'

'He's unlikely to have asked for help,' Sejer said. 'You could argue that was his responsibility. Many people have a miserable childhood: that doesn't give them the right to abuse others. On the contrary, they ought to know better. Or what do you think?'

'How easy is it to go to a therapist and say "Help me, please, I'm turned on by kids"?'

'No, that's not easy, I grant you. But life's hard for all of us.'

'I won't be able to get you to change your mind just a tiny bit?'

'No.'

'All I'm saying is that it's frighteningly complex,' Skarre said. 'What is force? Is it force to use deceit? Is it morally reprehensible to entice anyone into bed? Should we even be seducing one another at all? It's not easy being a man and getting to grips with all these rules.'

Sejer looked at Skarre across the table. 'I have no wish at all to discuss my private life,' he said, 'but following the rules has never been a problem for me.'

'I believe you because I know you. But imagine that you're a young lad in a dark, overheated room, surrounded on all sides by pretty girls flirting with you. You're tanked up with beer and hormones and your pulse is throbbing to the beat of the music. To make matters worse, you might even have taken an ecstasy tablet.'

'I wouldn't dream of it.'

'Of course not. But that's the reality we live in and my argument is that when it comes to our sexuality, we're struggling to catch up. We may think we're liberated, but it's only a façade. Research shows that we haven't come very far at all. Last night I sat down to do some reading. I wanted to know why some people become paedophiles. I didn't find any real answers because research has revealed almost nothing. There are individual triggers, but perhaps it's the case that nobody wants to know about this. No one cares about these men and certainly no one wants to talk about them; everything is reduced to universal contempt.'

'Well,' Sejer said, 'it appears you learned something after all, you're a mine of information.'

'Yes,' Skarre replied. 'And I was struck by how much can be accommodated within a framework of normality. I mean, as long as both parties are adults and consent. At the same time the world is full of people who have bizarre sexual fantasies, which they never carry out. And we should probably be grateful for that. And I've been thinking a lot about what Åkeson said. That we're dealing with a first-time offender.'

'We might well be,' said Sejer. 'So the question

101

is: will he be so horrified that he'll never reoffend or has he now developed a taste for it?'

After a short pause Skarre had another idea.'Now what about your grandson?' he asked, 'Matteus. Has he turned sixteen yet?'

'He's seventeen. Why do you ask?'

'He does ballet?'

'Correct. He dances classical ballet, and some people think that he shows promise.'

'Does he have a girlfriend?'

Sejer looked at him across the table.'There was talk of a girl called Lea once. I don't know much about it and I didn't want to intrude.'

'Has Lea turned sixteen?'

Sejer frowned. 'I don't know. Please don't add to my worries, I've got more than enough as it is. Matteus is a very sensible boy, and he is very conscientious in absolutely everything he does. He needs to be responsible, he needs to be the best. He needs to train harder than anyone so that no one can point the finger at him for anything.'

'He's ambitious?'

Sejer nodded. 'He needs to be, he's from Somalia. He needs to work twice as hard as everybody else, he has to defend his place on a daily basis.'

'I hear what you're saying,' Skarre said, 'but most people grew up with some sort of baggage. My father was a clergyman, he had very high expectations of me and he never got over the fact that I didn't want to study theology. Because of him, I've often felt like a failure. It has affected my entire personality that I was such a major disappointment to him, the knowledge that he went to his grave with his grief. If Matteus hadn't been black, it would have been something else that would haunt him his whole life.'

'I suppose you're right,' Sejer said. 'And the man we're looking for probably has an explanation as well, a reason for why it happened, for what happened to Jonas. But when you think about it, it's actually quite straightforward. We all have to abide by Norwegian law, every single one of us.'

CHAPTER 20

September 8th.

Edwin Åsalid was staring out of the window, waiting.

He noticed that the leaves were changing colour. They had gone from green to red and yellow. A light mist drifted across the houses and bathed them in a ghostly veil. Perhaps something evil is about to happen, he fantasised. His mother was busy cooking dinner when she heard a joyous squeal followed by heavy feet plodding across the floor. Edwin waddled into the kitchen, his big body quivering with excitement and anticipation. A sound pierced the silence in the house, the familiar ringing of a sharp, tinkling bell.

'It's the ice-cream van,' he pestered her. 'The ice-cream van's here! Please can I buy a box of choc ices, Mummy? Please, please?' He grabbed hold of one of her wrists and yanked her arm like a puppy pulling at a toy. Tulla Åsalid snatched back her hand and folded her arms across her chest. An expression of anxiety flashed across her face. Her son was morbidly obese and his weight was

103

increasing rapidly. He wanted ice-cream now, he was on his knees pleading with her, he shifted from knee to knee, his fists opening and clenching.

'Edwin,' she said weakly, 'we've talked about this.'

'But Mum,' he begged. 'Just one box!'

He gave his mother a beseeching look. Tulla Åsalid fought an inner battle. She remembered what the doctors had said, that she had to change his diet or his health would suffer and he weighed almost ninety kilos now. But he was imploring her, and she struggled to stay firm. Again he clasped her wrist, his brown eyes sparkling.

'There are twenty ice-creams in a box,' he pushed on, 'and there's hardly any fat in them because the ice-cream is made from powdered milk.'

Tulla Åsalid had to turn away. His brown eyes held their own power over her, she had to get away from them. She wanted to be strong, wise and consistent, but he was her child and the bond between them was as thick as a ship's hawser. She started to soften, intoxicated by his presence, weakened by the fact that he needed her, and she liked it when people begged her on their knees.

'How much is it?' she sighed.

'One hundred and twenty kroner,' said Edwin. 'It's a bargain.'

His choice of words made her smile. All the same it was with a heavy heart that she went to the kitchen drawer to find her purse. She pulled out a note and found some loose change in a glass. Edwin snatched the money from her hand and darted out of the house as fast as his fat legs could carry him. She went over to the window. She had lost yet another battle, but she was used to it. She spotted the large, pale blue van; it had stopped a short distance from their drive. And then she saw Edwin lumbering down the road like an overloaded ship. When he ran his chest appeared first, then his shoulders and his head, then the fat caught up with him, he rolled forward like a wave.

The driver got out of the van, smiling at the sight of the enormous boy. Tulla turned away from the window and went over to the mirror in the hall. She was slightly overweight herself, but fate had been kind to her and hidden it in all the right places. She had big, lovely curves, her breasts were perky and her hips broad, but she had a waist. She thought she resembled a beautiful instrument, a cello. Her hair was thick, blonde and shiny and she wore it loose even though she was forty. She wore a red dress and her curves were clearly visible beneath the thin fabric. She pressed her shoulders back and stuck out her chest, turned her head to check her profile. Her large nose gave her character, she had never wanted to change anything. Her brows gleamed brightly because she brushed them with oil. She snapped out of her reverie and went back to the window where she saw Edwin chatting to the driver. The man was an immigrant, Indian or Pakistani; she saw his teeth gleam white. The door to his van was open and the engine was running. I need to watch him, she thought, because Jonas August Løwe is dead and there's a man out there looking for young boys. But this was the ice-cream van and it turned up every other Thursday.

She went back into the kitchen. On the counter was half a kilo of minced beef; they were having

105

tacos and the man in her life was coming to dinner. She tried to calm herself down. She tried to follow a strategy because she did not want to lose this man, and as a result she put a great deal of effort into her cooking and her appearance. And even though they had never discussed marriage, he kept turning up. He was unable to resist her, and she did everything she could think of to keep him interested. She grew hot when she thought of him, yet she was also anxious because she could feel that he was not fully committed. And even though she was lovely, and even though she knew a few tricks in the bedroom, there was something reserved about him, a feeling of holding back she could not get to the bottom of. It takes time, she told herself, looking at the mince. He'll come round if I can just keep my cool. She could not imagine life without him: she started trembling as soon as she even visualised his face. He was tall, slim and blond. His body was taut and fit, and he was assertive in an attractive way. He never asked for permission if he wanted her, he just took her whenever he wanted to. She liked being possessed, liked that he forced her arms back and satisfied himself.

Again she snapped out of her daydreaming and went back to the window. She could no longer see Edwin. He had probably gone around to the other side of the van while the driver rummaged through the freezer for a box of choc ices. For a moment she stood there pondering her son's future. He was growing fatter and fatter and he was endangering his health. He was terribly shy with other kids. But he had some good friends, Sverre, Isak and Sindre. She thought of Sindre. A quiet boy with a frighteningly quick mind. He, too, felt like an outsider, he was simply too nice. She thanked fate for the boys who kept Edwin company. She adjusted the red dress and looked down the street. Her son was still blocked by the van. She did not understand why he was taking so long. She forced herself to stop thinking about it and returned to the kitchen where she fetched onions and jalapeño peppers from the cupboard, along with salsa, spices and tortillas. Soon she would hear the sound of Volvo tyres on the gravel and Ingemar Brenner would be on her doorstep, flashing his special smile. Again she grew hot. He was under her skin, she had his smell in her nostrils and when he was absent, when they were apart, her longing became unbearable. But he would be here in just a few minutes, and as she waited for him, she sashayed around like a young girl. Every time she passed the mirror, she smiled to herself, every time she reassured herself. This time it's going to last, she thought, he's the one, I'm feminine, I'm attractive and I surround myself with a cloud of wonderful perfume.

She returned to the window a third time because Edwin had not come back yet. The ice-cream van was still parked outside, the right indicator light flashing and the back doors open. Then she saw Ingemar's Volvo appear, he braked and turned into her drive. She rushed back into the kitchen, she started hyperventilating and forced herself to calm down. She was incapable of playing seriously hard to get, but she exhaled a couple of times to prepare herself. When she heard the doorbell, she walked calmly into the hall and opened the door. He was standing on the doorstep with his strong

107

arms folded across his chest. She returned his smile flirtatiously. It was as if they were playing a game, and how they loved to play, they consumed each other with their eyes, one second at a time. Then he crossed the threshold and entered the hall. He pushed her up against the wall and planted a hand either side of her head. Now she was trapped and she liked it; she closed her eyes. He smelled of aftershave and soap, and something else, something masculine. He kissed her on the lips. Then she opened her eyes and looked at him.

'Did you see Edwin?' she said abruptly.

'Edwin?' he said feigning ignorance.

She wanted to get out of the trap. He prevented her.

'I don't know anyone called Edwin,' he teased her. 'Come on, let's get cooking, Tulla.'

'We're having tacos,' she said enticingly.

He pursed his lips.

'I'll be having my pudding in bed,' he purred, rubbing his nose against her neck. Again she tried to free herself. She wanted to be in control, but her body grew weak. This was what he wanted and he was relishing it. Finally he stepped aside. She rushed outside and looked down the road where she finally spotted her son walking towards her. She rushed back inside the kitchen. Ingemar held up the packet of mince to his nose.

'Let's have it raw,' he suggested.

His words made Tulla giggle. Her laughter rose from deep inside her and rolled out into the kitchen, bright and joyous.

*   *   *

108

Edwin stopped in the hall, he did not know what to do.

He leaned his massive body against the wall as he held the frozen box away from his stomach. He heard his mother's loud laughter from the kitchen. It was as if she was in a different place and had severed the strong bond between them. It was Ingemar Brenner who made her laugh like that. He decided to wait until she had stopped, but there was something about the silence that followed. He was not sure what they were doing, and that, too, was awkward. Edwin had ended up buying a box of blackcurrant lollies because the ice-cream man had been out of choc ices. He heard the ice-cream van depart, the tinkling bells growing ever fainter. Again he heard his mother's laughter. He waited with his hand on the door handle. Finally he opened the door and walked in.

'Edwin,' he heard. His mum was coming towards him. 'What took you so long?'

'He didn't have any choc ices,' Edwin said. He looked shyly at Ingemar and he suddenly felt upset about everything, about being in the way and being fat.

'Can I have a lolly now?'

'Can't you wait till after dinner?' Tulla said in a long-suffering tone of voice.

His eyes grew shiny; he badly needed a lolly.

'Go on, let the boy have a lolly,' said Ingemar cheerfully.

Tulla surrendered to the men in her life. Edwin took out a blackcurrant lolly, tore off the paper and sank his teeth into it.

*   *   *

That evening they watched television.

Ingemar sat in the corner sofa with his feet up and Tulla sandwiched between his knees. Edwin sat in an armchair. The dining table was littered with wrappers and lolly sticks. He had already eaten four. In his hands he held a soft toy. It was a dinosaur filled with fine sand and he was stroking his lips with the tip of its tail. This repetitive movement induced a trance-like state in him. He was sated and felt a sense of calm, but it was never long before his hunger returned to torment him. The television seemed to be nothing but meaningless flickering. From time to time his mother's laughter would break through if anything funny happened on the screen. Ingemar was playing with her hair. When Ingemar was in the house, his mother became unavailable. Everything was better before Ingemar turned up, Edwin thought; fortunately, Ingemar had to go away a lot. His mother had explained to him that he travelled widely and gave talks to people. He would often call in the evenings and when he did, his mother sprang to life like a clockwork toy that had been wound up.

'Your homework, Edwin,' she suddenly burst out. 'Have you done your homework?'

She had finally remembered his existence. He hugged the dinosaur and shook his head.

'In my day we always had homework,' Tulla said. 'I don't understand what it is they're doing now.'

'We do it at school,' Edwin explained. 'We do it in the last lesson, it's called project work.'

'But then it's not homework,' Tulla said.

Edwin shrugged. Again he held up the dinosaur

110

to his mouth. He would be going to bed soon. Any minute now his mother would look at her watch, remember it was his bedtime and send him upstairs where he would lie listening to the voices downstairs: Ingemar's deep, calm voice and his mother's girlish laughter. Sometimes Ingemar would stay over and then he would hear them tiptoe down the corridor like naughty little kids. Other nights he would drive home and then Edwin would hear their voices on the doorstep. They always took ages to say goodbye. He preferred it when they went to their cottage, just him and his mother. Their little cottage named Pris which lay by Lake Sander. Ingemar never came with them and up there Edwin felt safe. And when there was no one else around his mother did not care how much he ate.

'Please can we go to Pris?' he asked.

'Not this weekend,' his mother said. 'Now charge your mobile,' she added. 'Do it right now. You're always forgetting to charge it.'

Edwin planted his hands on the armrests and pushed himself into an upright position. It was heavy going. He could feel Ingemar's eyes on his back as he went out into the kitchen. He was going to fetch his mobile from the bottom of his school bag, but he was distracted by the lollies in the freezer. The couple in the living room had already forgotten about him. He was acting on a mixture of grief and defiance as he gobbled down the lolly, standing by the kitchen window.

His massive body was clearly reflected in the glass.

CHAPTER 21

September 10th.

Edwin Åsalid was reported missing at seven o'clock in the evening exactly. By then Tulla Åsalid had been waiting for four hours, she had looked for him everywhere and she had wept. She had thought about Jonas August, and she was about to lose her mind.

'Paedophiles often follow a pattern,' Sejer said. 'They roam around, they carry out an assault and then they flee. I know what you fear, but this could be something else. There are many other explanations.'

Tulla Åsalid had been standing by the window. Now she turned around and looked at him.

'He's not able to move very quickly,' she said anxiously. 'I mean, if anyone's chasing him.'

Sejer and Skarre tried to understand what she was telling them. She went over to a chest of drawers to fetch a photograph. Sejer noticed that her hand was trembling.

'Take a look at this picture,' she said, 'and you'll know what I mean.'

They leaned forward to see. It was a full-length photo of Edwin with a small cottage in the background, and his reluctance to be photographed was obvious from his evasive eyes. He was without a doubt the largest ten-year-old they had ever seen. Yet there was something remarkable about him; he had inherited his mother's looks, his skin was pale like marzipan, his eyes large and dark. Despite his obesity, he was a handsome lad with big brown curls.

'Where does he tend to go?' Sejer asked. 'In his spare time.'

'They often go down to Loch Bonna,' she said, 'to Guttestranda. That was the first place I looked. I looked for them on the beach and on the jetty.'

'Is he able to swim?'

'No.'

'Has he ever been late before?'

'Never.'

She fell silent. They could hear how she swallowed.

'He tires easily,' she went on. 'If anyone offered him a lift, he would probably accept it because he's very unfit. He only moves when he has to, and he spends most of his time indoors, in front of his computer, munching something or other. So when he finally decided to go outside and get some fresh air I was overjoyed, despite what's happened, despite this business with Jonas, but he was meeting some friends and so I felt safe. I can't keep him locked up in here for ever. He sometimes sees Sindre or Sverre and Isak and I've tried calling them, but no one's at home at Sverre's or Sindre's, and Isak's parents are ex-directory. And, of course, I've been trying his mobile, but it was at the bottom of his school bag, I've told him time and time again that he must always take it with him, but he's so forgetful.'

She stopped to catch her breath.

Sejer stayed calm. They had speculated that this might happen, that another boy might go missing, but it had only been a police hypothesis, a scenario they had never really thought possible because it represented a type of offending which only

113

happened elsewhere, in other countries. Under corrupt regimes, places marred by poverty and desperation like Russia, where the kidnapping of young boys was large-scale.

'We need to take this step by step,' Sejer said, 'and it's possible that Edwin might come home while we sit here talking. We've seen it so many times and I'm sure he'll have a good explanation when he finally shows up.'

He could tell she was trying hard to believe him, that she needed a strong voice, an assurance which could stem this tide of fear.

'He hasn't had anything to eat for several hours,' she burst out, 'and he can't manage without food for very long!'

Sejer started wandering around the room. There were several photographs of Edwin on the walls, but they were not recent, and he could see clearly how his weight had increased year by year. One of the photographs showed Edwin as a toddler sitting on a man's lap, and he asked Tulla Åsalid about Edwin's father.

'He lives in Germany,' she replied. 'In Munich, he has a new family.'

It had to have been Tulla Åsalid who had ended the relationship, Sejer thought. She appealed to all of his senses and despite the circumstances she retained a sensuality which could not be ignored. He continued wandering around. The living room was elegantly furnished. She had several paintings on the walls, good ones too. There were oriental rugs on the floor, cream-coloured curtains, and a scarlet blanket had been casually thrown across the sofa. Behind all of this lay only one clear thought: everything was irrelevant now. They were nothing

114

but inanimate objects. Out of the corner of his eye Sejer could see Skarre making notes. Tulla listed names and addresses, she ran off to find more telephone numbers. She told them about Ingemar, her boyfriend. She had been trying to get through to him for hours and finally succeeded. When she heard his voice, she broke down completely.

Sejer looked outside in case Edwin appeared on the road, massive with his dark, curly hair. He had experienced it before, he had seen the passionate reunion between a mother and her child when all dark nightmares had been slain. That was how he wanted it to turn out, he beseeched fate for a happy ending. For one horrifying moment he imagined child number three going missing and how the pressure from the public and the media would make his world collapse. He imagined criticism and being incapable of making decisions, endless press conferences with barrages of questions and condemnation and sleepless nights. He looked at a shelf with books, his eyes scanned their spines. *Sons and Lovers* by D.H. Lawrence, *The Conquerors* by Roy Jacobsen, the Koran. On another shelf was a silver-plated infant's shoe and a piggy bank. His mobile started vibrating in his pocket and he answered it, still standing by the window.

'Yes,' he said, 'that's correct. No, he's still missing, we'll stay here until her boyfriend arrives, he's on his way and he'll stay the night. We're calling Edwin's friends at regular intervals, we're having trouble getting hold of them. We've got two cars out looking, but we haven't heard from them yet. Yes, we'll pop in. That's fine.'

He put the mobile back in his pocket. Thirty

minutes later they greeted Ingemar Brenner. Tulla collapsed sobbing in his arms. They said goodbye for the time being and headed back to the station. Five kilometres later they drove through the centre of Huseby. Skarre had a map in his lap and was trying to familiarise himself with the area.

'There's a new development to the west of Loch Bonna,' he said, 'and the roads there have quite unusual names. Someone from the council must have a vivid imagination. Listen to this. Detour and Shortcut. Sideline. First Exit. Last Exit. And this is the winner,' he said. 'There's a tiny little lane here called Naughty Corner.'

'I've heard of that one,' Sejer said.

'Where do you live?' Skarre joked. 'I live in the Naughty Corner and have done so all my life.' He folded up the map. 'I can't believe I just said that,' he said, embarrassed.

'Why not?'

'We might be dealing with an incredibly dangerous man and here I am making stupid jokes.'

'It's all right to have a bit of fun at work,' Sejer said. 'We don't need to feel bad about that.'

'Thank you.'

'It's just comic relief. Go on, if it makes you feel better.'

Half an hour later they were back at the police station. Skarre slumped in front of his computer as was his wont. Sejer started reading through his notes. Every now and then he would write a comment, a line to support why the evidence so far indicated that they might be dealing with a paedophile. You are weak, lonely and manipulative, he wrote, and you may be clever and

116

intelligent, but you lack empathy. You seduce small children, you tell them that what the two of you have is unique and special. Don't tell anyone. I'll take care of you. You'll get whatever you want.

He chewed the end of his pen for a while before carrying on.

If you're not caught, statistics show you will abuse up to one hundred and fifty children. And if you are caught and everything comes out into the open, all the children you've abused will feel terribly betrayed because they all thought they were the only one, the special one. That's when disaster strikes, that's when their world falls apart. And you have not only stolen their sexuality, but also their entire future and all the things you did to them will haunt them until the day they die.

He was startled when Skarre cried out.

'What's happened?' he asked.

'Ingemar Brenner,' Skarre said. 'Tulla Åsalid's boyfriend. I ran a check on him, just for form's sake, really, and there's only one person by that name in this area. He lives in Moløkka and he was born in '64. That sounds about right, doesn't it? That he's in his early forties?'

'Yes,' Sejer said. 'That sounds right. Why is he there?'

'He has two previous convictions. For fraud.'

'You don't say!' Sejer rushed over.

'Both charges were made by ex-girlfriends,' Skarre said. 'He conned them out of their savings.'

'Are we talking large amounts of money?'

Skarre read from the screen: '120,000 kroner in '96 and 210,000 kroner in '99. He got a custodial sentence on both occasions.'

'And where was he sent?'

'To Sem Prison.'

Skarre shook his head.

'He's in Huseby now, comforting her. And all the time his real interest is her money. If she has any. Should we get involved?'

'Yes,' Sejer declared. 'We should, but not tonight. For all we know he might have come clean about it to her; for all we know he might have turned over a new leaf.'

'Highly unlikely,' Skarre said.

'Let's make another call,' Sejer said. 'Try Mathilde Nohr's mobile.'

Skarre tapped in the number. She answered after four rings.

'The police.' She sounded taken aback. 'I see. What's wrong?'

'You have a son named Sverre?'

'Yes, that's right.'

He could hear that she was breathless.

'Is Sverre around right now?'

'Yes, he is. We're at my mother's, he's sitting in front of the television. What's this about?'

'Please would you ask him if he was with Edwin Åsalid today?'

'Edwin? Yes, of course. Just a moment please, I'll go and ask him, he's in the next room.'

Skarre could hear her voice growing more distant. Some questions and answers. Then she returned.

'He was out with Isak and Edwin,' she said. 'They went down to the loch. To Guttestranda.'

'Did they walk back home together?'

And this was when the penny dropped. He was a policeman calling to get information about Edwin. She was hit by the full force of what had happened at Linde Forest.

'Dear God,' she gasped. 'Please don't tell me he's gone missing?'

Again she had a muffled conversation with her son. Skarre could make out fragments, he heard the word 'police' and 'Edwin'.

'He was picked up by someone, I think, someone in a white car.'

CHAPTER 22

September 11th.

'Have you had a letter from your school?' Sejer asked.

'What letter?' Sverre and Isak looked at one another, they stood shoulder to shoulder in the doorway. Oh, yes, they had got the letter. They had read it together with the grown-ups and had a serious talk about what it meant. But the letter was about the car that waited outside the school, not the one seen driving down to Loch Bonna.

'Whom did you think it was?' Sejer said. 'Who picked up Edwin?'

'An uncle, maybe?' Sverre said.

'Does Edwin have an uncle?'

He grew nervous and shrugged.

'Did it look as if they knew each other?'

'They were talking through the window,' Sverre said.

His mother, Mathilde Nohr, pinched her son's hair at the back of his neck.

'Now pay attention,' she ordered him. 'This is really important.'

He nodded. He turned away defiantly because she had pulled his hair.

Sejer and Skarre drove the boys down to Loch Bonna.

'Why is the beach called Guttestranda?' Sejer wanted to know.

Sverre put on a precocious face. 'Because boys and girls weren't allowed to swim together,' he said; 'in the old days, I mean.'

'So is there a separate one for girls?'

'Of course. On the other side of Svart Ridge and though it's smaller, the sand is much finer and we can wade almost all the way out to Majaholmen.'

'What did you do while you were here?' Sejer asked.

'We sat on the jetty.'

'Did you see anyone?'

'There was a man taking four dogs for a walk,' Sverre said.

'Do you know him?'

'We don't know him,' Isak said, 'but everyone knows who he is because he's always out walking those dogs. His name's Naper.'

'Tell me a bit about Edwin,' Sejer asked them.

'He doesn't say much,' Isak said. 'He's too busy trying to keep up and he gets out of breath, especially when we're walking uphill.'

'He gets out of breath even when the ground is flat,' Sverre said. 'He gets out of breath if he as much as sees a staircase.'

'What did you do once you were on the jetty?' Sejer asked.

'We ate jelly turtles.'

'Jelly turtles. I see. Are they nice?'

'They're sour,' Isak explained. 'Edwin thinks

120

they're cool.'

Sejer surveyed the landscape. The beach was attractive. There was green grass, a jetty and some bathing huts. The bottom of the loch was covered with stones and, according to the boys, it dropped very deep further out. Three hundred metres with no warning, they explained.

They went on to the jetty and sat down, letting their legs dangle over the edge. They could see their own undulating reflections in the water.

'What were you talking about?' Skarre asked.

'We were talking about Alex,' Sverre said. 'We often do.'

'Who is Alex?'

'He's our teacher, at Solberg School. We're in Year Five and we have him for nearly all our subjects.'

Sverre brushed his fringe away from his face; his hair was coarse and the colour of copper.

'Do you like him?'

They glanced at each other.

'We like him,' Isak said, 'but he's weird.'

Sejer pondered their answer. 'Weird how?'

'He lives with another man,' Isak said. 'He's gay, you see. They both are. Alex and Johannes share the same house. And the same bed.'

They stared into the muddy water. The topic of conversation was making them embarrassed.

'How was Edwin yesterday?' Skarre asked. 'Was he like he normally is?'

'Oh, yes,' Isak said.

'How long was he here on the jetty?'

'I don't know,' replied Sverre. 'We weren't watching the time.'

'There's something important that we really

121

need to be sure about,' Sejer said, 'and that's the car. Was it someone you knew?'

They both shook their heads.

'Did the car stop down by the beach?'

'No,' Sverre said, 'Edwin started walking. They met each other near that substation up there.'

He pointed.

'Could it have been the same white car seen outside the school? Think carefully.'

'Might have been.'

'And you can't tell me what make it was?' Sejer asked.

'No, it was just an ordinary car.'

'Was there more than one man in the car?'

'No.'

Sejer looked out over the loch again. To his left, he saw the headland, a narrow tongue in the water.

'You told me that Edwin can't swim?'

Isak nodded energetically.

'He's let off,' he said, 'because he doesn't want to put on swimming trunks. Edwin doesn't do PE either. He can't manage to skip or jump over the vaulting horse. It's really hard for him to get up again if he falls over.'

'Does he get bullied a lot?'

They both shook their heads.

'No, Alex gets mad. He won't let us.'

*   *   *

They searched the jetty and the headland, but found no Edwin in Loch Bonna. Large, fat gulls screeched ominously at the search parties when they tipped out the rubbish bins in the area. The rubbish was scrutinised. Ditches, outbuildings and sheds were checked.

'What do we do now?' Skarre asked.

'We contact the council and get a list of all the residents in Huseby,' Sejer said. 'We get a list of everyone who owns a white car. Then we visit them and we interview them.'

'There are three thousand people living here,' Skarre said.

'I know.'

'Three thousand,' Skarre repeated as he pulled his mobile out of his pocket and started punching in the number. 'If we assume that each house has three inhabitants and that every household has one car, and many have two, we're talking about roughly one thousand cars, perhaps twelve, thirteen hundred.'

He continued punching.

'And if we assume, and I'm only guessing here, that every tenth car is white and I think that's a good guess, then we're looking at maybe one hundred and twenty people in Huseby who own a white car.'

'Then we've got our work cut out for us,' Sejer said. 'Everyone will need to be processed, I want them all entered on to a database. Ask them about their job and civilian status, how long they've lived in Huseby and check them against our records. And if it's at all possible, I want the officers to check if anyone walks with a limp.'

That night Sejer lay awake staring at the ceiling. He was scared of making a mistake, of overlooking or forgetting something. He was scared of relaxing or, for that matter, of falling asleep, because he would achieve nothing while he slept and he could not bear that. He lay awake imagining the man he was hunting. I'm coming after you, he thought, and I'm persistent. Even if it takes the rest of my life, I will find you and hold you accountable, because you have not only violated Edwin and Jonas August, you have violated our entire society. This you must understand: there is not a single soul in the whole world who will forgive you.

CHAPTER 23

Kristine Ris pulled her nightdress over her head, the thin fabric caressing her back. She wanted Reinhardt to touch her like this, but he never took the time, and so it remained something she could only dream of. A finger tracing her spine from her neck to the small of her back and making her shiver. For a while she stood naked on the bathroom floor. It was seven in the morning, and Reinhardt was already dressed. She adjusted the water temperature and stepped into the shower, she lifted her head against the warm stream as she played a game. She imagined she was covered by a layer of worries and now they were being washed away like dirt before disappearing down the drain. She could hear Reinhardt pottering about, she heard the radio in the living room. Security, she thought, that's why I stay, that's why I put up with it. Dear God, I'm like a child. What I have now isn't what I dreamed of, but at least I know what each day will bring, I can see what the rest of my life will be like. She jumped when the door to the bathroom was opened. Reinhardt pushed the shower curtain to one side.

'What's happened?' she said quickly.

Clumsily she covered herself up with the bottom half of the shower curtain. Reinhardt gave her an outraged look.

'He's taken another boy.'

'What? Who's taken another boy?'

'Well, we don't know yet, but my money's on that man from Linde Forest,' he said. 'The missing boy is from Huseby. There's total panic now.'

'No,' she said, baffled. She shook her head in disbelief. Her hair was wet and drops of water trickled into her eyes.

'Is that what they were saying on the radio?'

'Yes, I've just heard it. But they didn't give away many details, you know, they never do at this stage. But it's a ten-year-old boy and he goes to the same school as Jonas August.'

Kristine stepped out of the shower and grabbed a towel. She watched him with wide eyes.

'But where did they find him? Was he dressed?'

'No,' Reinhardt said, 'they haven't found him yet, they're still looking.'

'What do you mean they haven't found him?'

She took a smaller towel and wrapped it around her hair like a turban.

'Then how do we know what's happened to him?' she objected.

'Oh, they'll find him,' Reinhardt said, 'but by then it will be too late. Kristine! We're the only witnesses, the only ones to have seen him up close.'

Kristine got dressed. She was troubled by what Reinhardt had told her, by scenarios she did not want to entertain, by thoughts she did not want to think. They went down to the kitchen to have breakfast. Reinhardt made coffee.

'When I'm out and about I'll keep my eyes open. Just in case he might show up.'

Kristine took her usual place at the table. 'But what if you see someone, you tell the police and it turns out it's not him,' she objected. 'Imagine how awful that would be.'

'I really can't worry about that. If you think about it,' he added, 'not many people in this world can stop him from taking a third boy. But you and I can, we're in a unique position.'

It gives him a buzz, she thought, that it might be so.

She buttered a slice of bread.

'You might be right,' she said, 'but there's not much we can do in our unique position. Unless he shows up somewhere.'

'And he will, sooner or later. The question is: how many kids will he kill before that?'

'What's his name?' Kristine asked. 'The missing boy?'

'Something unusual,' Reinhardt said. 'Edwin. What a hopeless name for a small boy.'

She shrugged. 'He's probably named after someone. His grandfather, perhaps.'

'It doesn't suit him,' Reinhardt stated. 'Edwin is an adult's name. The name of someone who's fifty or sixty.'

'But he's going to grow up,' Kristine said. 'He's only a boy for the first ten years.'

She stopped talking. All he would get now was those ten years. She looked at Reinhardt. He seemed unperturbed. She had no idea what that signified.

'There's something about you men,' she said.

'Is there now?' He looked down at her. 'Why

don't you tell me what that is?'

'You're so simple.'

'Are we really?'

'If someone gives you a ball, you'll chase it for hours.'

'Ha ha,' Reinhardt laughed, he was finding all this highly amusing.

'You never stop playing. Whereas we girls, we grow up when we turn twelve, because we know we'll become mothers one day. One child can't take care of another, we have to be responsible.'

Reinhardt's smile stiffened and became acidic.

'Besides, our brains are very different,' she continued. 'I saw something about it on TV once. They had created this image, which highlighted the differences. Active areas of the brain were coloured red.'

'Good heavens,' Reinhardt chuckled.

'And inactive areas were coloured yellow.'

She swallowed another sip of her coffee. 'And do you know something?'

Her eyes met his across the table.

'The male brain showed just a small red spot,' she said. 'The active parts were limited to a small area. Whereas the female brain was almost entirely red. Because we're capable of thinking about many different things simultaneously,' she said triumphantly.

'While we focus on one thing,' Reinhardt said. 'And that's why we achieve more than you do. Whereas you busy yourselves with trifles and that's why everything you do is mediocre and half-hearted.'

The discussion was starting to make her dizzy.

'You're always the ones to stop when there's

127

been a road accident,' she said, 'or a fire. Or any other disaster, for that matter.'

'So what?' he replied. 'We like the adrenalin, Kristine: that doesn't make us inferior human beings.'

'That's not what I said,' she defended herself.

'I know you,' he said, 'and I know what you're thinking. But I don't mind admitting it. I'm interested in the missing boy from Huseby.'

She risked touching a sore point. 'Only a man who has no children of his own would say that,' she said.

He nodded. 'A good reason for not having any, wouldn't you agree? If you have a kid and then lose it, the rest of your life's ruined.'

'We can't think like that,' she protested.

He washed down his bread with milk.

'That is precisely how we should be thinking,' he said. 'Every eventuality must be taken into consideration. We have a child and he gets sick. Or we have a child and he is knocked down by a car. We could have a disabled child, born without arms or legs perhaps. We might have a badly behaved child. And we are left with the guilt and the shame. Or,' he concluded, 'we might have a child that gets murdered.'

'But why should that happen?' she said, aghast.

'Sweetheart,' he said, 'it happens all the time, and we're at the centre of it. You're hopelessly naive, you never think that such a tragedy could hit us. Do you really think we're that special?'

She brushed some crumbs off the table. 'But we have to concentrate on living,' she argued. 'If we always thought like that, we would never do anything, and we would never achieve anything.'

128

'I think like that,' Reinhardt said, 'and I enjoy my life.'

A pause arose. Kristine added sugar to her coffee and Reinhardt buttered another slice of bread. He had very forceful hands with coarse hairs on the back. She looked out of the window: on the small patch of garden a crow leapt about eagerly. She kept watching it. It struck her that she had never looked properly at a crow. It's pretty, she thought, and perhaps it really was a bearer of bad tidings, there was something mysterious about it, something secretive. Suddenly it raised its head and looked at her through the window.

Reinhardt interrupted her train of thought.

'He's got nothing to lose now,' he said. 'He's crossed the line. It might cause him to lose control completely.'

'You're just guessing now,' she said. 'Perhaps they'll find the boy alive and well.'

She swallowed a mouthful of bread.

'You're just being naive again,' he declared.

'I can't bear the thought,' she said, 'that a grown man would do that to a child.'

'You've always been so sensitive,' he said, 'but that's what I like about you.'

He got up from the table. As he did so, he gave her a look she had never seen before.

'If you ever leave me, I'll beat you to within an inch of your life.'

She wanted to laugh, but was unable to. Why would he say something like that? Two more crows had joined the first one on the lawn, they had settled by the hedge. While she sat watching them another two arrived and soon a whole flock had gathered.

'Look,' she said, pointing at the birds.

Reinhardt spotted them.

'They're eating something,' he said. 'I'll pop out to check.'

He disappeared out into the hall. She heard the door slam. More crows came flying, each one landing by the hedge. There was a mass of black and grey colour, she could see how they sat there pecking away. And she was reminded of a Hitchcock film she had once seen, *The Birds*. Then she saw Reinhardt walk across the lawn. The crows scattered and took off. He bent down to have a look, placing his hands on his knees for support: there was something in the grass and he was studying it carefully. He returned, smiling broadly.

'You ready then?' he asked. 'Time to get going.'

She got up from the table.

'So what was it?' she asked.

'A rotting badger,' he said, 'a huge, fat one, well over a metre long.'

CHAPTER 24

He looked out of the window, resting his palms on the broad windowsill for support. The farmer's mother was walking across the yard. Fetching eggs, he guessed. She had her arm stuck through the handle of an old-fashioned metal basket. It upset the rhythm of her walk and made her look less mobile than she actually was. He noticed that she was terribly bowlegged. She was bent double from age as well as gravity. He thought that if she were to fall, she would break every bone in her body. He pulled back a little so that she would not see him standing in the window. I'm a quiet sort of man, he thought, I don't draw attention to myself, and if I happen to meet anyone, I'm polite and respectful.

The old woman disappeared in the direction of the henhouse and he shifted his gaze to the hilltop. A car was approaching. It stopped by the letter boxes. Probably delivering his benefit cheque. He had been waiting for that. He went over to his sofa, sat down and fidgeted with his hands. I haven't been feeling very well, he thought, not at all well. It would have been nice to take a trip into town, but being recognised was now a serious risk. People were looking for him, they kept their eyes peeled. He could not relax until the evenings, when the darkness crept in around the cottage and yet another day had passed without the police finding him. He worried about what the police called their 'success rate'. He knew that they had allocated all their resources to finding him, that other offenders would escape because he was their priority. The police had announced that they would be carrying out door-to-door inquiries and his brain was working overtime trying to come up with a plan. But given that his name did not appear on any registers, surely he was safe, wasn't he? In order to bring him in for questioning they would need actual grounds for suspecting him, beyond the fact that he had happened to be in the area. He got up and paced the floor. He was restless and bursting with energy at the same time. To hell with them all, he thought, as his bitterness made his cheeks burn, to hell with everyone who doesn't understand.

When he relived what had happened, he felt a throbbing and an ache between his legs. At times it

131

was like a pulse beating all the way up to his tongue. Desperately, he prepared his own defence: the child had come on to him, had offered him a tantalising smile. And he was a good person, at least he wanted to be, and there was something strangely bewildering about lust, wasn't there? He remembered his mother walking in on him as he sat on his bed with no underpants on, playing with himself, almost absentmindedly. Something inexplicable had happened in the doorway. His mother had been overcome by a hysterical rage, her voice had contorted. What are you doing, what on earth do you think you're doing? Where are your manners, what is wrong with you?

He tried to relate his own actions to her reaction, but failed. Instead he was left alone with his lust and whenever his hands wanted to slip inside his trousers, his cheeks would start to burn. Every day with his mother was like being put through a grinder, he came out in thin strips. When she finally grew old, she would not die, either. For months she was confined to bed in terrible pain. He had sat patiently by her bedside, waiting because he did not want to miss the moment when she died. She groaned and screamed, she gurgled and rattled. For weeks and months, and every hour was filled with agony. He was unaffected by watching her, he felt neither joy nor relief, merely fascination. At long last she emptied her lungs in one final scream. 'That's enough!'

She spoke no more. Her chin sank down and her eyes stared at something beyond life.

He thought his fate was hard to bear. Others could love and follow their desires, but he was doomed to a life of celibacy, to fantasies that drained and tormented him. He would probably burn in hell for what he had done, he would burn in prison as well, no one would want to know him or talk to him after this. He thought about committing suicide and felt a stinging sensation underneath his eyelids. Perhaps it was best to end it all. He could go down to Loch Bonna one night, go out on the headland and let himself fall into the water. What did the future hold for him—nothing but contempt and condemnation? No money and no respect from the outside world? Not that he was much to look at, either, he didn't stand a chance with today's women, there was no end to what they demanded by way of appearance and success. And what was he? An ageing man with a limp and bad teeth, a man on benefits. He was not very adept at getting on with people. His social skills were poor, he did not understand the game and lost every time. Again he collapsed on to the sofa and stared at the old wheelchair in the corner from Plesner Medical Supplies. It had been his mother's and he should have returned it to the hospital, but he had never got around to it. It had been in his living room so long it had become part of his modest furniture. Now he got up and went over to it, lowered himself carefully into it. Clasped the wheels and felt the soft rubber against his palms. Something about sitting in the wheelchair made him feel he was in the right place. Of course he was disabled, he could not manage what others managed. He rolled silently and smoothly across the floor. All he needed was a blanket across his knees to make the illusion complete. Out of the corner of his eye he saw the newspapers on the coffee table, the photos and huge headlines.

Following Edwin's disappearance, the police considered him to be highly dangerous.

CHAPTER 25

'I've been reading about various types of paraphilia,' Skarre said. 'Experts have identified more than one hundred preferences. I can't deny that I'm fascinated. By the way,' he added, *'paidos* means boy and *philia* means love.'

'I know,' Sejer said.

'And there's another variant,' Skarre went on. 'Gerontophilia.'

'What's that?'

'Being attracted to old people.'

Sejer frowned.

'And acrotomophilia. A desire for people with missing limbs.'

'Is that possible?'

'It is. And of course there's necrophilia—'

'I know, I know. Let's change the subject. Can paedophilia be treated?'

'To some extent,' Skarre said, 'but the success rate is poor, on the whole. Ideally a person needs to be in therapy before they turn fourteen. And it's hard to make anyone do that. At this point very few will have started abusing.'

'But when does a person know that they're sexually attracted to children?'

'Early on. A conflict erupts between a child and its parents, an emotional conflict, and the child seeks a solution to it. The solution, that is, paraphilia, is one they usually discover between the ages of eight and nine, some as young as six. And over the years it grows stronger. There's very little research on the subject, that's the problem.'

'Go on.'

'In some states in the US,' Skarre continued, 'it is illegal to teach sex education to anyone under the age of sixteen.'

'Why?' Sejer wondered out loud.

'It's regarded as a form of assault. And consequently the system does not pick them up. And their paraphilia, if they have one, is allowed to develop unchecked. And even though we despise and reject what they do, their abuse is an attempt to solve a problem.'

'That part I understand,' Sejer said, 'but in this case I'm not prepared to make excuses for anyone.'

'There's another point,' Skarre said, 'which is worth considering. It's based on culture. We call it abuse, but what defines it as such? Religion? Morality? Experts, the authorities or we as individuals? In other cultures,' he went on, 'things go on which in Norway would meet with universal outrage and severe punishments.'

'Like what?'

'Polynesian mothers masturbate their young children to make them settle at night.'

'Good heavens.'

'Boys in New Guinea have to service older men in order for them to be regarded as real men. I won't go into detail about what they have to do; after all, you're easily embarrassed.'

'Thank you.'

'And then there are Portuguese grandmothers.'

'Are you about to slander Portuguese

135

grandmothers?' Sejer asked, appalled. 'I've been on holiday in Portugal, I've seen them close up, they're the very image of respectability.'

'They rub small boys in church,' Skarre said, 'so they'll sit still during evening mass.'

'I've never heard anything so outrageous.'

'But up here in the cold and freezing north there's really very little the law allows you.'

'We should be grateful for that,' Sejer said. 'We need to enforce it and we cannot have any grey areas.' He gave Skarre a stern look. 'If you put a child on your lap, there must be no ulterior motives.'

CHAPTER 26

Solberg School in Huseby was an old, yellow stone building surrounded by beeches. It was situated on a hilltop above Loch Bonna and those pupils whose classrooms faced north often daydreamed as they watched the blue water. Alex Meyer led Sejer and Skarre to Edwin's classroom. The room stirred mixed feelings in them, it had to do with the way it smelled, an indeterminate mix of food, green soap and children's bodies. Edwin's name had been written on the board in ornate letters and the pupils had drawn flowers and red hearts around it. But there was something else which caught their attention, something which stood out in the carefully organised room. A chair. A chair bigger and broader than the rest. It was obvious that Edwin was unable to sit at a normal desk.

Alex Meyer was a long-limbed man in his forties

with a mass of brown hair which had been left to grow as it pleased. Around his wrist he wore plaited leather bracelets and his trainers were bright blue with golden stripes.

'How are you getting on?' he asked. 'Do you think you'll be able to catch him? What do we tell the kids? Do you have any theories as to what's going on?'

Then he stopped himself, gave them a desperate look and gestured helplessly. He was slim and a touch feline, and when he spoke his whole body moved.

'As far as the children are concerned,' Sejer said, 'then you'll have to tell them that they'll find out the answer one day.'

Meyer went over to the window and looked down at the loch.

'Two boys from Solberg School,' he said. 'It's unbelievable. Do you know what the children are saying? That he's at the bottom of Lake Linde. That a dangerous man is loose in the forest up there. And I don't know what to say, because it might be true.'

Again Sejer had the feeling of standing empty-handed in front of a beggar.

'So what's the story?' Skarre asked. 'How's Edwin doing in school?'

Meyer managed a smile. 'In some ways I'm impressed that Edwin comes to school at all,' he said, 'because he's not doing very well. He's not very bright, and he struggles in all subjects. But when it comes to bullying, there's a lot of talk these days about children and how cruel they are to each other and I suppose that's true. But it has a point of origin. If they're used to being ill-treated at home, then they go out into the world with the same lack of respect for the feelings of others.'

'Do you have pupils here who are being ill-treated at home? Is that what you're saying?' Sejer asked.

'I've got my suspicions. Let me put it this way: I pay attention to what's going on.'

'Are you talking about verbal abuse or do you mean other, more serious types of abuse?'

'Possibly.'

'What about Edwin? Is he treated well at home?'

'I've no reason to think anything else,' Meyer said, 'unless you consider it to be a form of child abuse to allow a child to become morbidly obese.'

'That's a brutal claim to make,' Sejer said.

'It is.'

'To what extent can his difficulties at school be attributed to his obesity?'

'To a large extent, I would say. Many of his thoughts revolve around food. He finds it very hard to concentrate on anything else. Food comes first. It comes before playing, school and friends. Food is the first thing he thinks of when he wakes up and the last thing he thinks of before he goes to bed at night. He loves food more than anything else. But I help him as much as I'm able to, he's a very nice lad, gentle. It's bizarre,' he added, 'because in one way it scares me to see how quickly he gains weight, in another way it fascinates me. When he eats I can barely make contact with him. He grows distant and unapproachable, as if he were high.'

He went up to the board, took a piece of chalk and drew a small star above Edwin's name.

'So his weight,' Sejer said, 'is a major handicap?'

'It's worse than that,' Meyer said, 'it's life-threatening. Or it will be soon. Sometimes I think that he might have suffered a heart attack, that he's simply keeled over and you'll find him in a ditch.'

'What about his GP,' Sejer said, 'have you spoken to him?'

'Of course,' Meyer replied. 'I needed to know how to handle it. Edwin has always been allowed to do things at his own pace, I've never pressurised him. Naturally, he has been excused from PE. He sits on the floor watching the others while he eats one of his many packed lunches.'

Sejer studied the wall, which was covered by children's drawings.

'He's drawn a picture of his mum in a red dress,' Meyer explained, pointing. 'It'll be horribly empty if he doesn't come back. The pupils are distraught, they've lost everything they thought of as safe. Jonas August is dead and Edwin's desk is empty. The kids are barely allowed out of the house now, it's that serious. We've been asked to look out for the white car, but when the bell goes, it's total mayhem because everyone collects their children by car now. Before we start lessons every morning we talk about what's happening. However, we need to get some work done eventually, life has to go on somehow. But it's hard because their concentration is so poor. Some parents have told me their children find it hard to sleep at night. It's strange that it's happening here,' he said, 'in Huseby.'

'You're not immune from the rest of the world,' Skarre commented.

'How does Edwin deal with his weight problem, in terms of behaviour?' Sejer asked.

'I'm not sure I understand what you mean,' Meyer said.

'There are things he doesn't get. He doesn't move or exercise, he doesn't get good marks, he can only join in to some extent. Has he found some other way to make himself noticed?'

'Well,' Meyer said, 'at break time he often seeks out the adults. He'll say something nice and make himself as sweet as he can so that we'll like him, and we do. No one can say no to Edwin Åsalid with the brown curls. So in that way I can see how the wrong sort of man would be tempted.'

CHAPTER 27

Jonas August Løwe's funeral was held in Huseby Church and it was packed. What will the vicar say, they wondered as they found a seat in the hard pews; can he really find words for a tragedy like this? They doubted him on two fronts: they questioned his profession and they wondered whether he would manage to comfort them, though at the same time that was the reason they were here.

Sejer and Skarre observed everyone as they entered the church. Elfrid Løwe sat at the front. She was wearing a dark blue suit and the blazer-style jacket made her look like an adolescent boy. The vicar was standing in front of the altar with his back to the congregation. Conferring with God, Skarre thought, wondering if he would get any kind of explanation. Sejer noticed a couple in their sixties sitting either side of Elfrid; her parents, presumably. Her mother's Parkinson's was obvious, she shook uncontrollably. Jonas August's classmates sat in the pews behind them, each child very soberly dressed for the occasion. In contrast to the adults, who were all staring at a point on the floor, the children allowed their eyes to wander around the church with undisguised curiosity and they lingered on the coffin. It was strangely small and barely visible underneath the profusion of flowers. A hush of mourning filled the church, but there was something else, a sense of communal fear.

The organ began its swelling notes. I'm not a believer, Sejer reminded himself, so why do I feel joy at this sound? The organ? The vaulted ceiling with the angels? The stained-glass windows which filter the light beautifully across the pews? I find serenity, I find comfort. As though the absence of a God creates a void after all, but one I only become aware of when it's filled? He glanced furtively at Skarre seated next to him. He looked as if he was struggling with similar thoughts. What's harder, Sejer wondered: basing your entire existence on the divine only to doubt in a few moments of darkness, or embracing the beauty of a brief, earthly life before turning to dust, to dark nutritious soil? He was not an atheist, far from it, but neither had he ever believed that there was a God, externally or inside him. He had no awareness of any spiritual power. He thought that nature and mankind were physical entities which could be understood according to their laws and were by definition transitory. Surely their beauty

141

lay precisely in the fleeting nature of their existence? Of course he had experienced some glimpses of spirituality, moments which lifted him up and out of himself, moments that broke barriers, when he suddenly sensed something greater, like opening a curtain to let in the light. Like when his daughter Ingrid was born.

He looked down at the order of service, which the verger had handed him. There was a photo of Jonas August on the front, smiling cheerfully and revealing large front teeth. Then he raised his eyes and watched Elfrid Løwe, her short hair, her thin neck. Ever since her son had been found she had had to deal with so much. Shock and paralysis, fear and grief, identifying his body. Yes, that's Jonas. That is my Jonas. Finding an undertaker, choosing flowers and music and clothes for Jonas to be buried in, his pyjamas perhaps or a white shirt. She had talked to the vicar, she had tried to put words to her feelings. She had put a notice in the paper, she had chosen an outfit for herself, the dark blue suit. Now the vicar was about to take over and for a few hours she would be left to herself, no more practical things to think about. The rest of her life lay ahead of her, filled with long, black days.

The vicar looked out across the congregation.

'Today I'm angry with God.'

His statement made them sit up. Yes, that was to the point, surely that was what they all felt: anger and impotence? And who was God to say that this grotesque incident was part of His greater scheme?

'Today I'm angry with God,' he repeated, 'but I'm also filled with joy.'

Oh, Sejer thought, he's bringing in joy rather quickly, a tad too soon in my opinion. Again he

142

sneaked a look at Skarre sitting, as befits the son of a vicar from Søgne, with his straight back and his hands folded in his lap.

'For eight years Jonas August was a source of joy to us,' the vicar carried on. 'It was a brief joy, but who are we to count the hours and the days? Some people live short lives. Today we are gathered here to honour him, but it hurts. Today all we can see is evil and fear, the incomprehensible, the unforgivable, but with God's help we will one day see it in a different light. God will help us to accept this one day because he who took Jonas from us is a lost soul who has strayed.'

Has he now? Is that what's happened? Sejer thought, I'm hunting a lost soul who has strayed. No, that's not right. I'm hunting a man who puts his own desires before everything else, a man who cannot control himself, a man who will kill to satisfy his urges. When I'm at the police station interrogating him, there will be no room for acceptance. I will be polite and follow procedure, but I will offer him nothing: no mercy, no sympathy.

'Death is not final,' the vicar continued, 'because we are all on a journey, we will join this eternal river, it is the blood of all those who knew us and loved us and they will live on in us. We carry Jonas August. It is a heavy burden, but it will grow lighter. The tears we will shed in the months to come will turn into smiles. Do you remember Jonas August, we'll say, who was in our year at Solberg School? He always had a smile and a friendly word for everyone.'

He paused, lowered his head before raising it

143

again with authority and gravity.

'Death has arrived in his carriage. Jonas August has stepped on board.'

He paused again. The signs of good living and contentment showed in the potbelly underneath his cassock, but his face with its feminine features spoke of humility.

Then Jonas's teacher stood up to read a poem. The sheet of paper refused to lie still in her hands, it rustled so that everyone could hear and her voice threatened to break, but the words reached them all the same. They sent shivers down their spines.

Towards the end of the service the vicar asked the children to come forward. Each of them was carrying one long-stemmed red rose. They lined up in the centre aisle and stepped forward, one by one, to leave their flower on the coffin, twenty-three roses in all. It was impossible not to be moved by this image, the children, the roses and the coffin. Then they found their seats again and sat down happily on the wooden pews because they had completed their task. A task they had discussed at great length and, as they saw it, they had executed it with style and dignity.

Then something happened. No one was prepared for it. The vicar was shocked, everyone could see that. Some people clasped a hand over their mouth in fear, and Sejer felt an icy chill shoot down his back. Elfrid Løwe started to scream. The service had helped her maintain her composure, she had clung to the vicar's voice, but now she was screaming uncontrollably, heartbreakingly, a protest which made people jump in their pews. The screams came from deep within her and pushed their way out with a force no one would

144

have believed such a tiny woman possessed. For the best part of an hour the vicar had built a fragile construction of comfort and resignation. Now she tore it down. She screamed and she demolished it and people could no longer mourn with dignity.

'Come on,' Sejer whispered to Skarre. 'We're leaving now.'

The men left quietly and inhaled the fresh September air outside. Again they heard the organ, now muted behind the closed doors. Skarre fished out a packet of cigarettes from his dark jacket.

'My hands are shaking,' he admitted. He managed to light a cigarette and inhaled deeply. 'And if you dare to mention God right now, I'll leave.'

Sejer shook his head. 'No, but there's something else I want to tell you.'

'What's that?'

'Did you notice the man sitting in the last pew? On his own, wearing a grey suit, sitting closest to the wall?'

'No. What about him?'

'That,' Konrad Sejer said, 'was Reinhardt Ris.'

CHAPTER 28

The sight of Reinhardt in his grey suit was so unexpected that Kristine did a double-take. It was five minutes past four and her shift at the Central Hospital had finished. The Rover rolled smoothly to a halt at the front entrance, and she looked at him sitting in his best suit, she saw the white collar

145

and the wine-coloured tie.

'Why are you wearing a suit?' she asked. 'Where have you been?'

She got in and slammed the door shut. She folded her raspberry-red jacket and put it on her lap. Reinhardt eased the Rover past a stationary ambulance. An important smile played around his mouth, signalling that she would just have to rein in her curiosity.

'Didn't you go to work?' she asked.

He braked for a car coming from the right. He looks good, Kristine thought, he has long legs and broad shoulders and the suit fits him perfectly.

'Of course I've been to work,' he said, 'but I left early. I went to Jonas August's funeral.'

He speeded up as he turned out into the street. Kristine sat with her mouth hanging open. She could not believe her own ears. A myriad thoughts rushed through her head: he was nosy; or mad, even. A peeping Tom or, worse, a thief. Someone who stole other people's life experiences.

'I was curious,' he said calmly. 'I thought that a funeral of that kind would be different from any other funeral, and it was.'

'But you didn't know him,' she said. Again she felt outraged, as if he was some spoilt child she had to justify herself to.

'We found him,' he replied.

'Yes, but that doesn't mean we have to do anything, does it?'

'Perhaps not.' He hesitated. 'But it gives me certain rights, in my opinion. Think about it, sweetheart, we found him, we called the police, we waited, we answered their questions. We lay awake half the night.'

Kristine went over the recent events in her head. Next to her was a man who had finally discovered his purpose in life, a man who regarded other people's tragedies as entertainment, who thought that the murder of a child accorded him certain rights. This was the man she was married to, the man who had denied her what she longed for more than anything. She was bound to him until death did them part. She meant to keep that promise, but right now she needed to make a few demands of her own.

'Did you talk to her?' she asked.

'No, she was busy, so to speak.'

'Do you know what?' she continued, and she could no longer restrain herself. 'I would have understood you better if you had gone over to Jonas's mother, I mean after the service, and introduced yourself. If you had told her that it was you who found him. And that was why you were there. That would have been the mature, compassionate thing to do and it would have given her the explanation I think she is entitled to. But you sneak in just to get a cheap thrill from her tragedy and her grief.'

'I couldn't go over to her,' he said. 'I wanted to, of course, but it was impossible.'

'Why?'

His hands clenched the steering wheel. 'Because she started to scream. I've never heard anyone scream like that. I thought the stained-glass windows would shatter.'

Kristine gave him a shocked look. He was deathly serious now, as if the screaming woman had actually managed to upset his equilibrium. He increased his speed. She watched him out of the corner of her eye and it struck her that he would most probably never make a good father; he was too wrapped up in himself and his own affairs. This realisation made her feel uncomfortable and despondent. But I would make a good mother, she thought, and many are on their own with a child and they manage. I can manage, I can be strong if I have to. I want the love that others have, the love that lasts until death. I want it now. Yet again she peered at Reinhardt. He was happy to be who he was for as long as it lasted. He liked what he had, his job, his house and his car. I'm growing older, she thought, time's running out. These thoughts gnawed at her more and more. Slowly an idea began to emerge. She would do something irresponsible, she would quite simply deceive him. Help herself and take what she wanted. Men talked of female wiles, she told herself, well, I'll resort to those now. The thought of this made her heart beat faster and she feared her eyes would betray her plan. So she closed them and leaned her head against the headrest.

CHAPTER 29

He felt hungry, but he was unable to eat anything.

Not that there was much to eat either: the fridge was empty. A few times he opened the fridge door to look inside while he tried to find his inner resolve. He found none. On the contrary, he discovered as the days passed that his hunger seemed to protect him, he felt encapsulated by it as if it made him invisible to the rest of the world.

148

This feeling quelled some of his fear, because he did feel fear. He had pulled a chair over to the window where he rested his elbows on the windowsill, or he would sit in front of the television where he watched every news broadcast, the photos of the two boys glowing at him. Various experts analysed the incidents; all their theories were wrong. He was spending more time in the wheelchair, he experienced an odd joy rolling around in it. He rolled out into the kitchen to get some water, he rolled back into the living room and parked in front of the television. In the wheelchair he became someone else, in the wheelchair he was a geriatric with withered limbs, a poor thing you could not blame for anything. It was a relief to turn into someone else. He started going to bed early, it made the days shorter. Sometimes he had long, imaginary conversations with the police.

Listen to me, please, I can explain this!

Later in the evening, he would collapse in self-pity and shed bitter tears. If they became unstoppable, and this had happened, he would throw himself on the sofa, face away from the room and pull a blanket over himself. This is a dreadful existence, he thought, I'm a prisoner in my own home. I might as well be in prison, at least I would get a hot meal there and I could chat to the guards. He licked away his own tears, their salty taste awakened raw memories in him. He lay alone in the dark like this, but all the time coiled like a spring. He knew they would come and if he did not let them in, they would break down his door.

149

CHAPTER 30

They asked themselves these questions over and over:

Why can't we find Edwin? Is it a good sign that we haven't found him yet? Does it mean that he might still be alive? And if we're talking about the same offender, why has he taken the trouble to hide Edwin Åsalid while Jonas August was dumped beneath some trees? Was it possible for two paedophiles to carry out separate attacks in the same place in the space of one week? They thought of every possible scenario; absolutely every single permutation was examined. Were they dealing with a child suicide? Had Edwin's life been harder than the adults had realised? And if it was not about sex, what was the motive for a crime they could only sense the outline of?

A man called the station about some rumours which had started in Huseby and suggested that they might want to look into them.

'Joakim Naper,' Sejer said. 'Let's go and have a word with him.'

'Naper?' Skarre said. 'The man with the dogs? He's already been questioned.'

'I know,' Sejer said, 'but he has heard something. We've got to work with what little we have.'

*   *   *

The doorbell triggered fierce barking and they noticed claw marks on the woodwork.

150

'You've got to catch this man,' Naper said, 'and you'd better do it quickly.'

There was a violent commotion in the doorway as Naper yanked the dogs to one side and showed them to a living room with a view of the loch. The dogs had left their mark on the house and there was little left of the parquet flooring. His furniture was ancient and worn and some filthy brown strips of fabric hung by the windows, some sort of curtain supposedly. There were several photographs on the walls, all depicting dogs: dogs in the snow, dogs in front of a sledge, dogs on a beach.

'Yes,' he said, 'it's just me and the dogs here.'

He commanded the dogs to lie down. Sejer and Skarre found a space on a sofa covered in long, white dog hairs. Naper was a man in his fifties, short and heavy-set with an impressive iron grey beard, which he kept stroking. Whenever he looked at them, it was with brief, sharp glances; most of the time his eyes rested on the dogs.

'Like I told you. It's not much that I can offer you, I didn't see any people or cars the day Edwin Åsalid disappeared. But I saw the boys sitting on the jetty. Now the rumours have started. You might not have heard them, people don't like making accusations, they're scared they might be wrong. But I don't have any children at Solberg School so I don't care.'

He scratched one of the dogs energetically. The big animal rolled over on the floor.

'These rumours started before the boys disappeared. But now, of course, they've really caught on.'

Naper took his time. His hands were strong and hairy; they sank deeply into the neck of the dog.

151

'It's about a man who is gay,' he said, looking at them. 'And I'm not bothered by that, I've no axe to grind, live and let live I say. As long as you don't hurt anyone. Anyway, he lives with someone, has done for years, they live in Nordby where they bought an old house which they've done up. And to put it bluntly, a lot of young boys come to visit him.'

'Why do they do that?' Sejer asked.

Naper found an ashtray and took out a squashed packet of Petterøe tobacco from his shirt pocket.

'He's a teacher,' he said, 'at Solberg School.'

'Alex Meyer,' Sejer said.

'That's him. You've already heard, I thought you might have,' Naper said.

Sejer protested. 'Someone mentioned he was gay, that's all. Tell me how these rumours have come about.'

Naper rolled a misshapen cigarette, stuck it into the corner of his mouth and lit it.

'He brings the kids back home.'

'To his house?'

Skarre listened, his blue eyes fixed on Naper's face.

'No one's quite sure what goes on,' Naper said, 'or what part his boyfriend plays in all of this. But I do think it's odd that a teacher opens his home in this way. Sometimes the kids are there in the evenings. Don't ask me what they do, but I think that is strange. You'd have thought he would have had enough of them after a whole day at school.'

'Has anyone asked him?' Sejer asked.

'Don't know.'

'Do you happen to know the name of his boyfriend?'

152

'I do. Now, what was it? Johannes Kjær.'

Skarre made a note of the name.

Naper flicked the ash from his cigarette. One of his dogs gave a long yawn and Sejer caught a glimpse of its impressive fangs.

'Rikard Holmen, who runs the Kiwi shop, has two grandchildren in Year Five,' Naper said, 'and they've been to Meyer's house lots of times. But perhaps it's all above board. Perhaps it's just what I said it might be. Gossip.'

Again he bent down and started scratching another dog. Sejer went over to the window and looked down at the loch.

'You can see the jetty,' he remarked.

'Yes,' Naper said. 'I don't mean to boast, but this house, which I bought in '94, has the best view in Huseby.'

'Do you know Edwin Åsalid?'

'No. I don't know him, but I know who he is. Everyone does, he's hard to miss. And not that I know much about it, but I can't imagine what his mother thinks she's doing. The odd salad wouldn't have gone amiss.'

Skarre placed his notepad on the coffee table. 'Yes, if only it was that simple,' he said, flashing one of his dazzling smiles, as a result of which Naper missed his irony.

'I've tried to understand this thing about children,' he said. 'I mean, the men. Who want them. I suppose they actually prefer children. And sexual urges are strong, some perhaps can't control them. Like my dogs,' he grinned. 'But surely they've got a brain like everybody else, they must know that what they're doing is utterly wrong. They know it's a crime and that the children in

153

question are permanently damaged. How can they be so selfish?'

Sejer returned to his seat, the dogs watching him warily.

'It's the way of the world, a few people just take what they want,' he said.

'What are you going to do if he abducts another child?' He stroked his beard and gave them a challenging look.

'We'll continue to do our job,' Sejer said.

'I can't believe that it has ended like this,' Naper said. 'It was the last thing on my mind when I was out with the dogs. I noticed the boys when I was walking towards Svart Ridge because one of them waved. And because I used to be a photographer I paid a bit more attention to them. The light over Loch Bonna that day was amazing and I thought what a superb picture they made. Three boys huddled together on a jetty.'

CHAPTER 31

The leaves were falling from the trees, twirling slowly and mournfully. October brought black, cool nights. Sejer was busy with reports and witness statements. He studied the results from the door-to-door inquiries in Huseby, where anyone who owned a white car had been asked to answer a few simple questions. They had found nothing. They had gone through the registers of Ford Granadas and Mitsubishi Galants before checking out the rest of the district. They had accessed Autosys and searched for white cars regardless of brand. They initiated new searches. They even dragged Loch Bonna. This time they searched beyond the headland all the way to Svart Ridge but without success. They uncovered drains, they searched woods, they went into outhouses and down into basements.

At Solberg School the teachers struggled to maintain calm.

The days seemed like regular school-days, yet a state of emergency existed and everyone was allowed to speak if there was something they wanted to talk about. Trauma counsellors had advised the teachers to encourage the children to voice their thoughts, and as a result one boy suggested that Edwin might have been cut up since he had not been found. 'He might be all over the place in a million little pieces,' he declared precociously. His claim caused the other children to give him horrified looks. Others were adamant that Edwin was at the bottom of Loch Bonna. Others that he had been kidnapped and taken aboard a ship where he might be someone's slave and was being starved; perhaps he was now as thin as a matchstick and unrecognisable. Edwin's calm nature, Edwin's lethargy, Edwin's soft, modest voice had left a huge void and the pupils surpassed each other in praising him whenever his name was mentioned. Even though they had said things about him behind his back, even though they had mimicked the way he waddled and nicknamed him Fatty, they were on their best behaviour now and they genuinely missed Edwin. They were untroubled by their transition from mockery to tolerance. During lessons they would stare at his empty chair.

There was a greater degree of calm in Jonas August's class because the children there had attended his funeral. He was buried behind the church in the last row between the family plots of Haraldson and Ruste. On several occasions they had all gone to the church and stood in a semicircle around his grave thinking sad thoughts. A few stamped the ground in front of the headstone cautiously. They suddenly realised with awesome impact that he lay alone in the black earth, right underneath their feet.

Almost reluctantly the press turned its attention to other cases. True, they were not nearly as spectacular, but they were fresh. On the two months' anniversary of the discovery of Jonas August's body *Dagbladet* ran a major article about the boys. A unique case in Norwegian crime history, an extraordinary riddle for the police. Everyone feared that there would be a third attack.

'Time's passing,' Skarre said, 'and we can't even be sure what sort of crime we're dealing with.'

'Do you remember Helén Nilsson?' Sejer said. 'She, too, was ten years old. Helén Nilsson from Hörby in Sweden. She was found on a woodland road wrapped in a bin liner. It took police fifteen years to find her killer. Fifteen years and ten thousand interviews. We just have to keep going.'

CHAPTER 32

Reinhardt had fantasised about it countless times, the moment he would finally come face to face with the man from Linde Forest. And how that

156

moment would be filled with surprise and triumph. But he had never imagined that his heart would pound like this or that his cheeks would start to burn. It was the middle of December and they had gone to the ICA superstore to do their shopping. Reinhardt pushed the trolley and Kristine selected the groceries. She jumped when Reinhardt grabbed her arm.

'Kristine,' he whispered. 'Look!'

She tried to free herself. She had no idea what he was talking about, but she looked in the direction he was pointing and noticed a middle-aged man in a worn leather jacket. He was standing in the fruit section choosing some apples.

'Hans Christian Andersen,' Reinhardt whispered.

Kristine's eyes widened.

'It's the man from Linde Forest,' he said.

'Him?' Kristine asked. 'With the apples? No.'

'Yes,' Reinhardt insisted. 'You can see that it's the same man. Don't you dare tell me I'm wrong. Remember we saw him clearly, just a few metres away and in broad daylight.' He shook his head in disbelief. 'Bloody hell. And here he is now, doing his shopping, pretending nothing has happened.'

The man had his back to them, but then he turned and they could see his profile. Kristine could not believe that it was him; this man looked utterly pathetic and selecting a few apples seemed an insurmountable task for him. He would pick one up, turn it this way and that, put it back down, take another, his whole being seemed weary and wretched. She just could not imagine him being responsible for the murder of two children. She had expected someone evil because her mind had

157

embroidered on her actual experience and moulded him in the light of his crime. His eyes were blacker and his cheeks more hollow, that was how she remembered him.

'Just look at his profile,' Reinhardt said.

'He resembles him, that's all,' she declared, wanting to finish their shopping. She felt confused, she clung to the trolley. The man had turned away and all they could see was his back.

'It is him,' Reinhardt stated. 'We need to call the police.'

Kristine went over to the fruit section where she got some clementines. She glanced briefly at the man in the leather jacket and the memories came flooding back. She had to agree that he resembled him, but she still had doubts.

'I don't understand how you can be so sure,' she said. 'We only saw him for a few seconds and it was more than three months ago.'

'I'm certain,' he stated firmly. 'I'll never forget that face. Don't be silly now. This is what the police have been waiting for all this time.'

The man headed for the checkout.

'He's limping,' Kristine said.

'Exactly,' Reinhardt said. 'He's dragging one leg. Now do you believe me?'

Kristine was overcome by a sudden, inexplicable fear. She did not like being near him. She hated that he walked around all ordinary looking, buying apples like normal people.

'We've got to find out if he drives a Granada,' Reinhardt said. 'I bet you he does. Hurry up, we can't lose him!'

'I haven't finished my shopping,' Kristine objected.

158

'That's not important right now,' Reinhardt snapped.

They followed him at a suitable distance. He went to the checkout and placed his shopping on the belt.

'We'll take the checkout next to him,' Reinhardt said, 'otherwise he'll finish before we do. You pay and I'll pack!'

He slipped past her and waited while the cashier scanned their groceries. Kristine paid and they left. They quickly loaded their shopping and got into their car, where they waited for him. Shortly afterwards he appeared with a carrier bag in each hand.

'Do you see a Granada anywhere?' Kristine asked.

No, Reinhardt thought, no Granada, but he could have been wrong about the car. He did not say so out loud because he hated being wrong. The man was now heading towards a white car.

'A Carina,' he exclaimed. 'An old Toyota Carina. It looks like a Granada from the back, I should have known it was a Carina! We must get a look at the number plate. Do you have something to write with, Kristine? We'll get his registration number and give it to the police. Hurry up. For God's sake what are you waiting for?'

She fumbled around in her handbag for a pen and some paper while the man put his shopping in the boot of his car. There was something slow and hesitant about him, as if everything was an uphill struggle. Kristine scribbled down the registration number on a scrap of paper.

'We'll follow him,' Reinhardt said.

Kristine gave him a dubious look. 'Surely we

don't need to follow him,' she said, 'we've got his registration number. All we have to do is call the police.'

But Reinhardt was unstoppable. 'I want to know where he lives,' he said. 'I have to know. Look, he's turning right, I bet he's from Huseby. He's speeding. And he's not indicating either. What a crap driver.'

Kristine groaned in despair.

'If he turns off, we have to let him go,' she said. 'It's not our business to follow complete strangers to find out where they live.'

'I don't have a problem with following him,' Reinhardt said. 'Later we'll call the police and give them his registration number, his address and everything. Jesus Christ,' he exclaimed, punching the steering wheel. He was so excited his cheeks had gone bright red.

'You could be wrong,' Kristine said.

'Not this time. Admit it, he looks like him, he's the spitting image.'

'He does look like him,' she conceded. 'But people resemble each other.'

'He's limping,' Reinhardt continued.

'So does my uncle,' Kristine said, 'because he's got a tumour in his knee.'

'Now stop being so stupid,' he raged. 'You agreed with me, don't you dare back down now!'

They followed him for eleven kilometres. He took the exit for Huseby precisely as Reinhardt had predicted. The car went through the town and turned left at the top of a steep hill.

'Granåsveien,' Reinhardt said. 'I bet he lives at Granås Farm. Perhaps he rents a cottage there.'

'We can't follow him all the way to his house,'

Kristine protested. 'It might ruin everything if he sees us in his mirror. I don't think the police would be best pleased to know that we're playing detectives.'

'I'm bloody well not going to turn around now,' snarled Reinhardt. 'I want to know where he lives.'

The car stopped by a row of letter boxes and the man got out.

'He's opening the middle box,' Reinhardt said.

The man got back in his car and drove down to the right, where he stopped outside an old cottage.

Reinhardt drummed his fingers on the steering wheel.

'He's noticed us,' Kristine said. 'He's realised that we've been following him.'

'He's gone inside now,' Reinhardt said. 'Now get out and find out what the name on the letter box is.'

She got out of the car and ran over to the letter boxes. She stood there for a few seconds before running back and getting into the car.

'His name's Brein,' she said. 'Wilfred A. Brein. Can we go now, please?'

CHAPTER 33

The following morning Reinhardt leapt out of bed to listen to the morning news. There was no mention of the case. He ran to the letter box to get the newspaper, leafing through it feverishly, but there was nothing about the man from Linde Forest, no announcement that the police had finally received the vital tip-off and made an arrest.

161

That meant one of two things. The man had been interviewed and eliminated, or they had botched it. Had they not taken his call seriously? The very thought outraged him, and, having paced up and down the room a few times, he called the police station.

A female officer answered.

'All tip-offs are followed up,' she said, 'but it takes time. We're still getting a large number of calls.'

'But this is not just any old tip-off,' Reinhardt said, his frustration turning his voice shrill. 'It's about the man from Linde Forest whom you've been wanting to speak to since the fourth of September. My wife and I found the body of Jonas August, and we were the ones who saw a man in a blue anorak by the barrier. Wilfred Brein from Huseby. Have you interviewed him? Does he have an alibi?'

'I can't give you that sort of information,' she said curtly, 'but I have made a note of your call and it will be followed up.'

'Listen,' Reinhardt said. 'Please would you find out if anyone's been to see him? The police have been known to make mistakes. A killer will walk free if this information is lost in the system. Please don't make that mistake, it would be awful for you.'

He heard a sigh at the other end.

'All right. I'll find out. You'll have to wait a moment.'

He waited. Kristine was standing next to him now. She, too, was waiting.

'It's unbelievable,' he said, 'that they can faff around like this.'

162

'They've got to follow procedure,' Kristine said. 'They can't bring people in just like that.'

'Here I am trying to be a good citizen,' Reinhardt fumed, 'but if they can't be bothered to take the public seriously, they'll pay for it. I'll go to the press.'

'Hundreds of people have called,' Kristine said. 'You're just one of many.'

Being thought of as one of many did not appeal to Reinhardt. He scribbled something on a notepad. *Bloody murderer*, Kristine read.

'Hello? Are you there?'

'Yes. What did you find out?'

He let go of the pen and straightened up.

'There's obviously been a big mistake,' the officer said.

'What kind of mistake? How?'

'I've found the report,' she said. 'We sent a car to Wilfred Arent Brein yesterday. To number 3 Granåsveien in Huseby.'

'Yes?'

'He's in a wheelchair.'

Reinhardt gawped at Kristine.

'What are you saying? A wheelchair?'

'He's a wheelchair user,' she repeated.

'No, I'm sorry, but you've made a mistake. We saw him in the superstore, he was doing his shopping and he drives a white Toyota. Listen, you really have made a mistake, my wife and I both saw him walk. He limps slightly on one leg, that's all. Jesus Christ.'

He huffed irritably.

'Let me talk to Sejer, please,' he demanded.

'He's out,' she said, 'but I've made a note of what you've just told me. I'm sorry, but we're terribly busy and we just can't waste time on incorrect information.'

Reinhardt slammed the handset down.

'A wheelchair?' Kristine said in disbelief.

*　　　*　　　*

I could leave him, Kristine thought, I could save up some money and rent a bed-sit somewhere, I could do that. He has to let me go. I can't stand this life any more, I hate that he never listens to me.

Feeling despondent she let herself fall into a chair. Reinhardt had been thwarted and she had no idea what he would do next. God knows where he is, she thought, and what he's up to. She felt her life had become impossible after the 4th of September; something had been unleashed in Reinhardt, something unknown to her. He had gone out and the house lay quiet, it was the calm after a storm.

She tried to imagine living on her own and how lovely it would be. Decide everything herself, reclaim her body, fill her life with good things, a child perhaps. Never having to hear his overbearing voice, feel his constantly domineering presence. Then she imagined Reinhardt's reaction and recoiled. If you leave me, I'll beat you to within an inch of your life, he had said. His words had terrified her, but she had dismissed them as a joke. He wasn't like that, he couldn't be.

She felt a surge of anger because the police had failed to catch the man who had taken the two boys. She started pacing the floor, a constant, restless walk. From time to time she would look out into the road, but there was no sign of the

Rover. She looked at his desk where he normally sat with his back to her. What should I take with me if I go? she thought. Some clothes, some books, any important papers. My passport, she thought, where is my passport? In the drawers of Reinhardt's desk, perhaps? She could not remember which one it was and had to go through each drawer. They were all crammed with stuff. They need sorting out, she decided, as she went through old letters and Christmas cards. There was no sign of her passport. Perhaps Reinhardt had put it in his file. He had one where he kept all their important documents, an accordion file with multiple compartments. She found the file, opened it and went though each compartment looking for her passport. She found her marriage certificate and for a long time she sat staring at it. She had married him. She had believed she was doing the right thing.

She continued and came across user manuals and the paperwork for when they bought the Rover. And finally she found her passport, in its protective red plastic folder. She squeezed it hard. Then a large yellow envelope caught her attention. She opened it and looked inside. It contained a photograph. She sank on to the floor and placed it on her lap. It was a photograph of a girl of five or six with straight dark hair and a fringe. She had a big gap between her front teeth. Kristine had never seen her before and her brain struggled unsuccessfully to place the girl. A little girl. How weird. And there was something else which disturbed her. The photo of the girl was a headshot and her shoulders were bare. Then it hit her. He has a daughter, she realised, with another woman and that's why he doesn't want to have children with me, because he already has one. And he's probably paying child maintenance to her. She gasped for air. She planted her palms on the floor for support. She returned the photo to the envelope the way she had found it, as her mind started to freewheel. What if he was one of them? She barely had the strength to voice her fears in her own mind. One of those who abused children. No, not Reinhardt, it was a ludicrous thought, almost hysterical. But the little girl with the naked shoulders, what was that about? She took the photograph out of the envelope and studied it once more. She did not look like Reinhardt, in fact, she did not even look Norwegian, her eyes and hair were so dark. She put the photograph back in the envelope, put the envelope back in the file and placed her passport in her handbag. She sat down on the sofa to wait and looked out of the window at the fading light. Then she went to the bathroom and stared at herself in the mirror. She clutched the sink as she slowly counted to ten. It could not be true. She was tired and wanted to sleep, but she did not want to go to bed, she was unable to relax. She kept seeing the child with the naked shoulders and her strange, almost pleading, eyes. She started demolishing her marriage. Everywhere she found something she had previously overlooked, tiny, ugly signs. In bed he often displayed a mixture of distance and brutality. He lives in this house with me, I can't stand it any longer. It's wrong. I've lost my way. She lay down on the sofa wishing it would swallow her up. She lay there watching the hands of the clock on the wall.

CHAPTER 34

'Why are you sleeping on the sofa?'

Reinhardt's voice cut across the room.

'Where have you been?' she gasped as she struggled to sit up. She held the blanket against her chest as a form of protection because he was a different Reinhardt now, someone she no longer knew.

'I went for a drive,' he said indifferently. 'I needed some fresh air.'

'It's almost two o'clock in the morning,' she burst out. 'You've been gone for hours.'

'I needed some time on my own,' he said. 'Now calm down, sweetheart.'

'You could have told me,' she replied. 'I would have understood.'

He went into the kitchen, opened the fridge and returned with a can of beer in his hand.

'I don't have to be accountable to you for my every move,' he said, lifting the can to his lips. She folded the blanket neatly and got up from the sofa.

'I'm going to bed,' she said. Her voice was strained.

'You're not looking at me,' he said suddenly. 'Are you angry about something?'

She could not think of an answer. All she could think of was the photograph in the folder. What would Reinhardt say if she confronted him with it? No, she did not dare, he was very tall and broad as he stood there in front of her.

'There's no need to make a drama out of it,' he said. 'I'm here now and you managed to have a nap

167

on the sofa. It's really no big deal.'

'Goodnight,' she said, heading for the door.

He sat down and put the beer can on the coffee table with a bang.

'You're really quite sweet,' he said softly, 'but you can be a bit uptight.'

She turned around and looked at him. 'I'm so sorry,' she said tartly. 'But I had no idea where you were or what you were doing. I'm going to bed now. That sofa is not very comfortable to sleep on, but I was too worried to go to bed. But I will now. Goodnight.'

She went out into the hall and ran up the fifteen steps to the bedroom. She rarely told him off and she was scared now. She crept underneath the duvet where she listened out for sounds coming from the ground floor. All she wanted to do was go to sleep, but she felt wide awake. Her eyes sought out the darkness in the room she knew so well, the room they had shared for many years. It was only a question of time before Reinhardt would come up the stairs and lie down next to her. She did not know if she could bear to have him so close, given what she knew now. And if he tried it on, she was scared that she might scream, yet at the same time she thought about the child she so desperately wanted.

I won't give up until I've got what I want, she decided. And there's only one way. She lay there waiting with her eyes open.

CHAPTER 35

One day Sejer and Skarre drove to Linde Forest.

The road up there was narrow and steep with hairpin bends, the unstable verges offering little protection from the sheer drop down to a brook at the bottom of the ravine. The Highway Department had created a passing place halfway up, but they met no one on the five-kilometre drive. At the top was a small car park with room for three to four cars. Sejer pulled in and stopped at the red-painted barrier.

'This is where they saw the man in the blue anorak,' he said. 'Reinhardt and Kristine Ris. Right here by the barrier. There's no doubt that they got a good look at him. It was sunny on the fourth of September and visibility was fine.'

'But how does that help us,' Skarre asked, 'when Ris orders our officers to go and look for a man who turns out to be in a wheelchair?'

'I don't understand it,' Sejer said. 'Something must have happened. A mix-up. We need to look into it.'

The men began to walk. They left the path and wandered between the spruces until they got to the spot where Jonas August had been found. The memory of the half-naked boy was still vivid in their minds.

'He'll refuse to explain himself,' Skarre said. 'His defence counsel will advise him not to say anything.'

Sejer smiled briefly.

'He feels he's the victim. Poor me, I have such

169

strong urges, I just can't control them.' Skarre's voice was dripping with irony.

'He's only trying to solve a problem,' Sejer said. 'We agreed that, didn't we?'

'He drove along the road,' Skarre said. 'He abducted a child, it's inexcusable.'

For a while they looked around. The hush from the tall trees put them in a reflective mood. Skarre walked towards the pile of logs where Kristine Ris had sat on the 4th of September. He sat down and lit a Prince cigarette.

'But all the same,' he stated firmly, 'he's not feeling good. He probably doesn't have a moment's peace. He is frightened to death at the thought of the hatred, the shame and the newspaper headlines. It might even kill him.' He inhaled deeply. 'People do die from things like that.'

Sejer sat down next to him. 'We expect to love and be loved,' he said, 'but paedophiles are supposed to control themselves. Saying that, love is never straightforward for any of us. Everybody seems to be breaking up these days.' He stopped talking at this point, he was entering unfamiliar territory. 'What about you, by the way? Still single?'

Skarre smiled broadly. 'Why would I need a wife,' he quipped, 'when I've got you?'

*   *   *

Later they drove to Guttestranda and sat on the jetty. For a while they savoured the unique feeling people experience in the presence of water. Sejer tried to glimpse the bottom, but failed. Then they

170

saw a man walking along the beach some distance away.

'We have a visitor,' Skarre said.

The man had a brisk, energetic walk, he was short of build and bald, and he was wearing a navy blue puffa jacket and faded jeans. He raised his hand and greeted them solemnly. He reminded them of a little kid bursting with exciting news.

'My name's Andor,' he said. Sejer and Skarre looked at him with interest.

'You're detectives,' he stated.

They nodded.

He took a few steps closer to them and crouched down. He smiled confidently. His skin was strangely smooth and clear as if life had left no trace on him.

'I live in the yellow house up there.'

He turned around and pointed. 'The big one with three storeys. Behind that long balcony is my bedroom. I've just noticed I've left the window open. I'd forgotten all about that. I hope it doesn't start to rain or my bed will get soaked.'

Sejer and Skarre looked at the yellow house.

'It used to be a railway station,' he explained. 'The railway line went all the way down to the water.'

'Really?' said Sejer. He studied the man who had introduced himself as Andor. He estimated him to be around forty, he had small, chubby hands with stubby fingers and a budding beer belly. Was he mentally disabled? Sejer wondered. No, not that, just different. Someone at ease inside his own kingdom where he reigned supreme.

'I live with my mother,' Andor explained.

Skarre smiled broadly. Andor was obviously on

171

benefits.

'Mother cooks,' he said, 'and I earn the money. I see people, every day, between ten and two o'clock.'

'You see people?' Skarre frowned.

'They come from all over eastern Norway. There are all sorts of things wrong with them. I have warm hands.'

'You're a healer,' Skarre exclaimed.

'Correct,' nodded Andor. He planted his hands firmly on his hips, exuding pride in his own abilities. He looked superior.

'How exciting,' Skarre said generously.

Andor looked at Sejer, his eyes sharp now. 'You suffer from psoriasis,' he stated.

Sejer's eyes widened.'Yes,' he gasped, 'you're right. How did you know?'

'I can see it,' he said simply. 'And it's bad right now. Because you haven't been able to find Edwin.'

'I'm impressed,' Sejer said. 'Yes, it's particularly bad right now. Do you have any advice for me?'

Andor nodded calmly.

'You need to move your chair,' he said. 'The one you sit in every evening.'

'Move my chair?' Sejer said baffled. 'But I like where it stands, by the window. That way I have a view over the city.'

'Well,' Andor said. 'I didn't say you had to move it to the other end of the room. Just shift it a bit. The point is to get you out of the space you're in now and into a different one.'

Sejer nodded obediently.

Andor walked to the end of the jetty where he stood for a while watching the water. He made no

172

sign of wanting to leave or to chat. He stood there like a statue, yet it seemed as if he was offering them something. After a while Sejer worked out what it was.

'Did you know Jonas and Edwin?' he asked.

Andor turned around slowly. 'I know everyone in Huseby.'

Sejer scrambled to his feet. He walked to edge of the jetty and stood next to him.

'Where should we be looking?'

Andor looked up at the considerably taller inspector.

'I know it sounds a bit strange,' he said, 'but I'm only telling you what I'm seeing. It's up to you what you make of it.'

'What do you see?'

'Hasselbäck,' he said. 'That's all. I think about Edwin and the word Hasselbäck appears. I found it on the map, it's in Sweden. In Västmanland.'

Sejer frowned. 'Are you telling me that someone's taken him to Sweden?'

Andor became irritated. 'No, that's not what I'm saying,' he said. 'That's your interpretation. I see what I see. You can't expect me to tell you what it all means.'

He turned abruptly and walked quickly up towards the yellow house, leaving the two now somewhat bewildered men to sit down again.

'Hasselbäck,' Skarre said pensively. And then looking at his superior. 'Do you believe people like him?'

Sejer shrugged.

'Yes,' he said after a pause. 'I believe they see things. But then again, we all do, we just don't attach any special meaning to them. Fancy him

173

knowing about my psoriasis, though. What are the chances of that?'

'So if Andor's right,' Skarre said, 'then Edwin might be in Sweden. Or his killer might be from Hasselbäck, or Edwin might have been taken to Hasselbäck, dead or alive.'

Sejer fixed his eyes on a small island some distance away.

'What are you thinking about?' Skarre asked.

'I'm thinking about Tulla Åsalid,' he said. 'I've spoken to her parents and they're worried. They told me that Tulla has changed since she started seeing Brenner. That Edwin came second. That they had never seen her so crazy.'

'Crazy?'

'That's how they put it. And it's all very well that two people love each other, but the greatest love should be reserved for our children. They are the ones we would die for. Wouldn't you agree?'

'It's been known for a mother to kill her children to get a man,' Skarre said. 'Do you remember that case in the States? A mother of three became infatuated with someone, but he wasn't thrilled at the prospect of taking on her three children. So she put them in her car and rolled it off a jetty.'

'I think Edwin's disappearance is about something else,' Sejer said.

'But Brenner might be a man like that,' Skarre said.

'A man like what?'

'A man who wants Tulla, but isn't interested in Edwin.'

He took a few steps, stopped, then raised his hand to shield his eyes from the sun.

174

'Talking about love,' Sejer said. 'Look at that little island out there. It's called Majaholmen. It reminds me of another island, in Hvaler, called Gunillaholmen. It's nothing but a few rocks and some windswept pines, but it was the scene of an ancient and horrific love story.'

'Enlighten me,' Skarre said.

'The fjord is filled with shallows beyond Gunillaholmen. Gunillaholmen itself is a desolate place and it's not even named on the map, but it got its name after Gunnhild Taraldsdotter. At the start of the seventeenth century she gave birth to a child in secret, you know, in the fields. She killed it, of course, out of sheer desperation, fearing the shame and the punishment that went with having an illegitimate child. You know how they thought in those days.'

Skarre nodded.

'But the body of the baby was found soon afterwards, though by then it had been partly eaten by swine,' Sejer continued. 'The poor, wretched farm girl confessed immediately and was arrested. The judges unanimously agreed that she should be decapitated and her head put on a spike as a warning to others. It was placed on the island where it stood for fifty years. The seagulls stripped her skull in less than a fortnight.'

'What about the child's father?' Skarre wanted to know.

'His name was Jon Mickelsen,' Sejer said, 'and he was let off with a fine.'

For a while they were both silent.

'I've always believed that crime stems from desperation,' Sejer said. 'Conditions in the sixteenth and seventeenth centuries led many to

175

kill their infants; now there are very few cases because single mothers are treated far better. We've never had it so good, yet the number of crimes committed has soared.'

'Desperation takes many forms,' Skarre suggested.

'Yes,' Sejer said, 'I suppose you're right. And sometimes I imagine that our offender is someone who stands on the sidelines, watching life from a distance, like it's a party to which he hasn't been invited.' This notion made him think of Edwin. 'How much do you remember about being ten?' he asked.

'A lot,' Skarre said. 'I was in Year Four. I sang in the school choir and I had a crush on a girl called Else. We had a mean arrogant teacher. His name was Lundegård. I've no time for stupidity, he used to say, if we got low marks in a test. He talked a great deal about World War Three, about how we should prepare ourselves for it. Don't be naive, he would say, because it's going to happen. My heart used to skip a beat every time I heard an aeroplane.'

Skarre slammed his hand on the edge of the jetty. 'How about you? What do you recall?'

'We lived on Gamle Møllevej, outside Roskilde, in Denmark,' Sejer reminisced. 'The house was white with blue shutters and in the summer it was overrun by hollyhocks. We kept bantams and it was my job to collect their tiny eggs every morning. And we had a wire-haired dachshund called Ruth. My mother had a small ceramics workshop, where she made pots and little sculptures. Our house was filled with them and she liked giving them away to people who came to visit us. I did well at school, but I was rather shy. We had a nice teacher, Mrs Monrad was her name. She was an inspiration. What do you think? Are there still people like her around today?'

'Some, but they are few and far between,' Skarre declared. 'Alex Meyer may be one such teacher. And that might be why the rumours started to spread. He's too good to be true, people begin to doubt his motives.'

'Meyer doesn't have a record,' Sejer said. 'I've checked him out.'

'I would expect you to,' Skarre said, 'but there has to be a first time for everything. And the people who hurt us are more likely to be someone we know rather than total strangers. He might have had a thing for Edwin. He gave him a special chair and placed him at the front desk.'

'Perhaps he did that to protect him,' Sejer suggested.

'Possibly. I'm merely passing on my observations,' Skarre said. 'You told me to look out for the little things.'

They fell silent once more and gazed out over the loch, towards Majaholmen.

'Can you feel that icy wind?' Skarre asked. 'We're not going to find Edwin before the frost takes hold.'

'What do you think Maja did wrong since she's got her own island, too?'

'Can you see that church spire on the other side of the loch?' Sejer asked.

Skarre nodded.

'She had been to a christening and was rowing back across the loch when her boat capsized, right by the island. She was wearing national costume

177

and it dragged her down.'

He got up to leave. 'Think about it, a waterlogged national costume weighs as much as a grown man. Ah, well. Edwin in Sweden? Highly unlikely. But there's no harm in listening to good advice. Anyway, it's time for me to go home and move my chair.'

CHAPTER 36

Two boys sat hunched over a fifteen-hundred-piece jigsaw. The image was a battle scene, Stamford Bridge in 1066, when Harald Hardråda fought Harold Godwinson. The battle was slowly taking shape in front of their eyes, but there were still many blood-soaked pieces to go. One boy had found a severed arm, the other was holding a head. They had worked on the jigsaw for weeks. The horses and soldiers were in place and dark, dramatic clouds were forming in the sky. Alex Meyer stood silent, leaning against the wall with his arms folded across his chest. He was watching the boys with interest, but looked out of the window with an alert gaze when a white Mazda slowly rolled on to the drive. Seconds later his boyfriend appeared, but he did not say hello to the boys. Instead he went straight to the kitchen with two carrier bags.

'Nice to see you,' Alex called out.

Johannes took the groceries out of the bags. He still had his back to him.

'How was your day?' Alex was still smiling.

'Same as every other day,' Johannes replied.

178

'Every day the same trepidation when I get home. Wondering if the house is packed with those kids of yours.'

Those kids. Alex looked into the living room.

'They're called Oscar and Markus,' he said, 'and I like having them in the house.'

'Yes, that much I've noticed, they've been coming here for months. But if you've got any sense of responsibility, you'll put a stop to it. People are talking.'

'You're not responsible for me and my actions,' Alex said, 'and of course people are talking, we're not like them.'

Johannes gave him a reproachful look. His dark hair was cut short and Alex could see the rounding of the back of his head above his slim neck.

'Don't talk rubbish. Of course it affects me too. It's great that you're a star teacher, but you don't have any reason to get involved with their free time.'

Alex sat by the kitchen table.

'So what's the problem, Johannes?' he probed. 'Do you feel threatened?'

Johannes said nothing. He smoothed the carrier bags and folded them neatly before putting them away in a drawer, but he refused to sit down. The fact that he was still standing underlined how important this was to him.

'Two boys have gone missing and people are looking for a scapegoat. They said in the papers today they might have been abducted by someone who knew them. I really think you need to take this seriously. Everybody knows this house is overrun with kids and they're beginning to wonder why.'

'Children need to relax,' said Alex. 'So much has

179

happened and I have to do something. They sit with that jigsaw for hours, Johannes, it's good for them, it teaches them patience and discipline, and kids today don't have much of that. Listen to how quiet they are.' He nodded towards the living room.

'And I sneak in a bit of history. If their parents are worried, all they have to do is call and we'll have a chat about it. And since nobody has been in touch I'll take it as a sign that everything's fine.'

Johannes shook his head. 'You don't understand how sensitive this is,' he said. 'There are some ugly rumours going around.'

'Perhaps it's all in your imagination?' Alex said. 'You think people are out to get you, that they're going to take something from you, but they're not. You need to learn to take it easy.'

He placed his elbows on the table. He was starting to feel angry. 'Life's wonderful, Johannes.'

Johannes started cooking dinner, but his abrupt movements gave him away. Alex returned to the living room, to the boys.

'How are you getting on?' he asked. 'Who's winning?'

'Godwinson,' Markus said.

'Godwinson is wiping the floor with Hardråda.'

'What are you doing at the moment, do you have a plan?'

'We're collecting all the bloodstained pieces,' Oscar said.

'And afterwards you can collect all the pieces with iron,' Alex said. 'Then all the pieces with water. All the pieces with sky. Be clever about it, have a system.'

The boys found the pieces and put them into

piles.

Alex held up a severed arm and described with gruesome detail how the wound would have been cauterised with a red hot iron in order to stop the bleeding.

'Imagine the sound,' he said, 'when the iron sank into the severed arm. It hissed like meat in a frying pan.'

'Is Johannes cross?' Markus asked. He looked towards the kitchen.

'He's not cross,' Alex smiled. 'He's scared. Scared of everything that might happen, but never does.'

The boys nodded.

'Do you want some casserole? Johannes has just started making it.'

The boys were not entirely sure what casserole was, but they said yes.

'So who tidied up afterwards?' Oscar asked. 'Who would pick up all the arms and legs? Who buried the dead horses and the dead people?'

Alex shrugged. 'I don't know. But I imagine they had a way of taking care of it in those days, after all, there were so many battles. But it was a tough age and you're very lucky to be alive today.'

He returned to the kitchen to help Johannes with the cooking, took a leek, found a knife, and started cutting it into thin slices.

'They're safe and utterly engrossed in the jigsaw,' he said. 'They're best friends. They're hungry and soon they'll get a hot dinner. Life's really quite all right,' he said. 'Life's better than people make out, Johannes, and people are better too.'

Johannes turned and looked at him. His short

181

hair ended in a long diagonal fringe.

'You know how to talk, I'll give you that,' he said in a resigned voice. 'But life's not a picnic, and you can't trust people. And I worry that you're about to learn this the hard way.' He put water in a pot and added the vegetables, the lid rattling as he put it on.

'But that's why you love me,' Alex smiled. 'You've been with me for ten years and you've never regretted it.'

'Oh yes,' Johannes replied, 'I've regretted it. God knows I have. I'll never be able to match you when it comes to joy and optimism.'

'But I've never expected that,' Alex said. 'You should be yourself, but you shouldn't worry about things that haven't even happened. It will make you ill and stressed and old and grey before your time. Hand me the pepper, please. Let's make sure the boys get something warm inside them.'

'I still think you ought to think about what you're doing,' Johannes said. 'You bring your pupils to your home after school. You play with them, you feed them, and in the evening you drive them home. And it's always the boys, Alex.'

He looked sternly at him. 'There has never, ever been a girl in this house. I think you owe me an explanation for that. After all, you teach girls as well, don't you?'

Alex shrugged and sat down. For a while he scratched the kitchen table with his thumbnail.

'Of course,' he said, 'but I get on better with the boys. Or, I don't know, I've never really thought about it. You're making mountains out of molehills. Haven't you ever heard of chance?'

'Yes and I don't believe in it. If the police come

182

knocking, you're on your own.'

'The police? Oh, please, get some perspective,' Alex said. 'Are you ashamed of me?'

Johannes looked away.

'That's it,' Alex exclaimed. 'You're ashamed of me. You're ashamed that you're gay, you're ashamed about everything. And all the good things in life are passing you by.'

'I'm not ashamed. But there's a child-killer on the loose and people are talking about you.'

Alex got up from the table. He went over to Johannes, leaned against the worktop and sighed. 'It's not like we're ever going to have children of our own,' he said.

'Why would we want to have children?' Johannes said. 'We've already got a house full of them.'

'But I've always wanted a son, that's all.'

Johannes had been dicing vegetables. Now he stopped and slumped a little over the worktop.

'Did you bring in the post?' Alex asked.

Johannes put down the knife.

'Yes,' he said quietly. 'I brought in the post, I always do.'

He picked up the knife again and carried on.

'Where did you put it?'

No reply.

'Johannes,' Alex said. 'Did you put the post on top of the fridge?'

He tried to fathom Johannes's reluctance. On the top of the fridge he found a pile of junk mail, a few letters and a small picture postcard. It depicted a boy and a girl picking flowers on the edge of a cliff and behind them stood an angel with white wings. There was something profoundly touching

183

about the image and for a moment Alex felt as if he was the guardian angel, that he would never let his pupils out of his sight. Perhaps someone else had thought exactly the same and this was their way of showing their appreciation. He turned over the card and read the message. There was a name, an address and a few brief lines.

'Well?' Johannes asked.

Alex turned his back to him and Johannes could see that he was clasping his mouth with his hand.

'It's from the Parents' Association,' he stuttered. 'They've asked for a meeting.'

CHAPTER 37

Granås Farm consisted of a farmhouse, a storehouse, two cottages and a barn and three hundred and fifty acres of farmland. An avenue of tall birches led up to the farm and you could see that the wind from the loch had taken its toll on the treetops. The icy air hit Sejer and Skarre as soon as they got out of their car. In the hollow below they could see an old cottage. It was dilapidated, but it could be argued that it still retained a peculiar charm of its own. Some thriving, but untidy scrub grew along the walls and a fine layer of snow covered the grass surrounding the cottage.

'What do you think?' Sejer asked.

'Don't know yet,' said Skarre.

The men walked around the cottage until they found the entrance marked by two old wooden posts covered by dried hops. Sejer looked at the

184

farm. He saw the old greenhouse with its broken windows, a stationary tractor and a black cat slinking through the snow. A Toyota Carina was parked inside a lean-to of corrugated iron next to the barn. It was well maintained for its age and it was white.

'He may or may not be in a wheelchair,' Sejer said, 'but he does drive a car. And why hasn't he had a ramp installed to his front door? How does he get up and down the steps?'

He turned to Skarre.

'Who were the officers who interviewed him the first time?'

'Don't know.'

Sejer looked towards the kitchen window. He could swear he detected movement behind the curtain, a face that quickly retreated. He went up the steps; nothing happened. He deliberately fumbled loudly with the door handle, then he waited, before knocking several times. Finally they heard noises from within. The door was opened slightly and a man peered out. The sharp light hit his face and caused him to squint. His hair was grey, almost straw-like, his skin was pallid and in dire need of some sunshine, as it had a bluish tint. He was sitting in a wheelchair, an older model, his hands resting on its wheels.

'Wilfred Brein?' Skarre asked.

The man scowled at them. His shirt, faded and worn, was hanging loosely outside his jeans. On his feet he wore brown leather slippers whose stitching was coming apart. But it was something else that caught Sejer's attention. The man's resemblance to Hans Christian Andersen was striking.

'Police,' Sejer said. 'We would like to come

185

inside for a few minutes.'

Brein measured the men with his eyes. 'Why do you want to come inside?' he snarled. He kept his hands on the wheels as if, at any moment, he might reverse and slam the door.

'Just a routine visit,' Sejer assured him, 'in connection with a case we're working on. We have a few questions, it won't take long.'

Brein jutted out his chin. He clearly wanted to signal something, they were just not sure what because he looked so pathetic. Besides, there was something about his legs which aroused Sejer's suspicions. His thighs were muscular, they showed no sign of wastage.

'It's to do with a witness statement,' Sejer said. 'There's something we need to clear up.'

'A witness?' Brein said curtly. 'What do you mean witness?'

'Witnesses claim to have seen you in Linde Forest. On Sunday the fourth of September in the afternoon. They saw you as you passed the barrier. You were heading for your car. I know it's been a long time, but I'm asking you to think back.'

Brein's face became closed, his pallid cheeks turned hollow.

'I know it's difficult to remember after all this time, but might they be right?' Sejer asked.

Brein rolled his eyes theatrically.

'You're barking up the wrong tree completely,' he muttered. 'Haven't you got eyes in your head?' He banged his fists against the wheels of the chair.

'Please excuse me,' Sejer said, 'but I presume that you only use your wheelchair occasionally. And that you have better days when you can get about unaided. Given that you have also been seen

186

in the ICA superstore, and furthermore you drive an old Toyota Carina. Which hasn't been adapted for wheelchair use. Or has it? Do you mind if I check?'

He nodded in the direction of the Toyota.

Brein grimaced. 'I walk with great difficulty,' he maintained.

Sejer nodded sympathetically. 'Precisely. But there are clearly exceptions. Perhaps the fourth of September was one of them, perhaps it was one of your better days and you went for a walk in Linde Forest.'

'I couldn't possibly go for a walk with this hip,' Brein said, placing a hand on his right hip and giving Sejer a look of suffering.

'It was crushed by a Volvo on a pedestrian crossing. The joint is stainless steel and it aches.'

'I see,' said Sejer, still being exquisitely polite. 'But there may have been something you needed to do up there?'

'Which case is this?' Brein asked. His eyes had become evasive now. They flickered around the farmyard, to the barn and the stationary tractor.

'Jonas August Løwe and Edwin Åsalid,' Sejer said. 'We've appealed for you to come forward in the newspapers and on every TV channel, several times. To put it plainly, we've been looking for you for nearly four months.'

Brein placed his hands on his knees. He had large hands with yellow fingernails.

'I read about it in the papers,' he said. 'About the two boys.'

He tried to get comfortable in the chair and did so with exaggerated effort.

'They were in all the papers. Huseby was

invaded by journalists for weeks. I don't see how it concerns me, what all this fuss is about. This is the second time you've come knocking on my door. And I've told you all I'm going to tell you,' he added.

'Did you go to Linde Forest on the fourth of September?' Sejer asked him.

'I have been known to drive up there,' he said. 'People up there would recognise me because I used to live on Linde Farm when I was a boy. We rented the brewer's cottage.'

'Did you see two people?' Sejer asked. 'A couple in their thirties, right by the barrier?'

'Are you deaf?' Brein yelled. 'I wasn't there on the fourth of September. My hip was playing up.'

Skarre took a step forward. 'You were seen,' he said firmly.

Brein tightened his grip on the wheels. 'Your witnesses are mistaken,' he said.

'Please let us in,' Sejer persisted. 'Let's have a talk. You're very important to us because if you were up there, you might have seen something that can help us.'

'I saw nothing.'

'They noticed that you walk with difficulty,' Skarre said. 'Because you do, don't you?'

Brein shrugged.

'I'm not the only man with a limp around here,' he retorted.

'Of course not,' Skarre said. 'But we have good reason to believe that it was you. It's to do with your appearance. What was your business up there, can you tell me something about that?'

Brein fished a packet of cigarettes out of his shirt pocket. The men followed his movements as

188

he stuck a cigarette in his mouth. He found a disposable lighter and inhaled greedily.

'Well, what might a man be doing in a forest,' Brein speculated. 'Berry-picking, perhaps?'

Sejer made no reply. The fact that Brein had lit a cigarette might mean that he was prepared to continue talking to them, so they stayed where they were.

'No, honestly, I don't go to the forest very much,' Brein said casually. The cigarette glowed against his pale face.

Obviously he's a suspect, Sejer thought, he confirms all our prejudices. All the same, he might be innocent. We must proceed with caution.

'If you happen to think of anything later,' Sejer said, 'something you need to tell us, we would really like you to get in touch.'

'You don't say,' said Brein.

Sejer considered the disturbing fact that they had no grounds for interviewing him. He had been spotted in the relevant area, but he had no previous convictions and there was nothing that linked him to the crime. I've only got one card left to play, he thought, and I've got to play it now.

'However, there's an easy way,' he started, 'to put an end to this. But it requires your co-operation.'

'It would be a relief to get this over with,' Brein said.

He was angry now. Angry that they harassed him when his life was already filled with anguish and misery.

'It so happens,' Sejer went on, 'that we have obtained some evidence. And with your help we can eliminate you.'

189

'What are you talking about?' Brein asked suspiciously.

'You volunteer to give us a saliva sample.'

A deathly silence followed. Brein's eyes narrowed.

'I refuse to be treated like a criminal,' he exploded.

'A DNA test would also prove your innocence,' Skarre argued.

'I haven't killed those boys,' Brein raged, 'and that's God's honest truth. I've got nothing else to say to you!'

He flicked the cigarette away and reversed the wheelchair back down the hallway. He struggled considerably to shut the door, but after several clumsy attempts he finally managed to slam it.

Sejer and Skarre looked at each other. They were both grinning broadly.

'What do you think the court will say?' Sejer said.

'They might throw it out,' Skarre suggested.

'They might,' Sejer said, 'but we're not doing anything illegal.'

'No.'

'And evidence gathered in this way would be admissible in court. Wouldn't it?'

'And no one can claim that we lied to Brein. Or entrapped him.'

'No, they can't.'

'We've just had an incredible stroke of luck. And what if we get a match?'

'Then it becomes his defence counsel's problem,' Skarre said. 'Let's risk it.'

'Let's risk it,' Sejer agreed.

He squatted down and looked closely at the

cigarette Brein had tossed aside.

'Do you have an evidence bag?'

CHAPTER 38

Sejer looked at the photographs of Edwin and Jonas August.

'Have you considered that it would take three Jonases to make one Edwin? Jonas weighed twenty-eight kilos. Edwin weighs nearly ninety.'

Skarre studied the boys. One tiny and skinny, the other huge and obese. 'Just as well the public can't see us now,' he said, 'sitting here, making fun of the boys. Where are you going with this?'

'I'm not making fun of them. It's a fact.'

'But is it relevant? That they are extremes?'

'I don't think it means anything in particular. They were walking along the road when he drove by. They both got into his car, which might mean that they knew him. However, I doubt that they would know Brein and that's why I hesitate. And I'm not buying the wheelchair story.'

'Surely people don't have a wheelchair in their home unless they need it?' Skarre protested. He felt restless. He started pacing the floor. 'What if Brein does a runner while we sit here twiddling our thumbs.'

'We're not twiddling our thumbs,' Sejer said, 'and I can't imagine that he is going anywhere with that bad hip of his. You need to calm down. You're pinning everything on him. Don't do it: you could end up terribly disappointed.'

Skarre walked to the door. 'Come on,' he said.

191

'We're going out. We can walk and talk, I need some fresh air. It's got to be him, it's got to be Brein. I can't bear another dead end, not after all this time.'

They went out into the city. A little more snow had fallen, a fine powdery layer. The sight of the snow made them feel ill at ease. They thought of Edwin Åsalid and images of a frozen body started taking shape in their minds.

'So you think Brein's our man?' Sejer said. 'Does he confirm all our prejudices?'

'He's on benefits,' Skarre said. 'He's a loner. He has little money, dresses badly, finds it hard to interact with adults. Rather scruffy, a bit of a loser. Yes, of course he fits the profile. But there might be another side to him, which so far we've failed to see. Something noble, even, what do I know?'

'Something noble? Why noble?'

'I don't know. I just don't want to be prejudiced, though I think it's probably too late for that. You saw him too, you must have formed an impression?'

'We're all prejudiced,' Sejer said. 'It's a vital part of our survival instinct. What did you think when we were standing outside Brein's front door? Your gut reaction. Be honest.'

'I thought that it might be him. That he might have killed Edwin and Jonas August. What did you think?'

'That he might be innocent. We've got to be very careful.'

'I knew it,' Skarre said. 'You're a better person than I am.'

A few snowflakes had landed on Sejer's grey hair. His sharp profile stood out clearly against the

192

white background.

'We have nothing to fear, we live in a country with a decent legal system,' he said. 'If it turns out we have a DNA match, Brein will have access to a defence counsel and anything else he might need. He will be treated humanely and given plenty of time to tell us his side of the story. Jonas August won't have that privilege and neither will Edwin. They have lost the rest of their lives, and their deaths were horrific. They were alone and they were terrified. I think about that a great deal.'

'I try not to,' Skarre admitted. 'The thought of it chills me to the bone.'

'It has its uses,' Sejer said. 'You need to keep the crime in mind and remember how evil it was. And for that matter, the role we play in all this.'

'Which is what?'

'Well, you know,' Sejer said. 'We get involved and we restore order and dignity.'

'Good heavens,' Skarre exclaimed. 'That's beyond us. All we can do is clean up, Konrad.'

'Don't underestimate yourself or your own purpose.'

'What do you think the prosecutor will say?' Skarre said.

'That Jonas August died in particularly aggravating circumstances. And that the punishment should reflect it. But the man in the dock, if we end up with a man in the dock, will be preoccupied with saving his own skin, and that's his right. But I can't stop myself from saying that a little remorse would be appropriate. There is not enough remorse in Norwegian prisons. And remorse would help the victim's family. Mankind can be very magnanimous, given the chance.'

'Is that your honest opinion?'

'It's a belief that sustains me.'

Skarre bent down and scooped up some snow in his hands, pressing it together into a rock-hard ball.

'Here we are waiting for the results of the DNA test,' he said, 'and Brein is pottering about in blissful ignorance. I can't stand it.'

CHAPTER 39

Elfrid Løwe had come to the police station where she spent a long time talking to Jacob Skarre. He listened with kindness and attention, resting his chin on his hand.

'Jonas was a quick and gentle boy,' she said. 'Nimble like a squirrel, up and down the stairs like the wind. Curious, eager and positive. Sometimes he would look at me with his large, blue eyes, hungry for love. He needed so much attention, and I could offer him an endless supply, it was just the two of us. At school he was quiet and shy, his teacher was always telling me so at parents' evenings. Jonas is a little passive, she said, it would be good if he could try to be a little more assertive in lessons. He suffered from a number of allergies, but he managed his medication himself. I thought it was going well on the whole, but I always worried about his asthma. And he was tiny. Perhaps that's what held him back. I'm sure you'll start growing soon and you'll be big and strong in a few years, I used to say. Mothers always say things like that because we can't bear our children's

194

disappointment when something upsets them, it tears us apart.

'But he was as good as gold, well-behaved and polite, so if an adult asked him to do something, I mean, like get into a car, because I suppose that's what happened, well, he would have got into the car because he was so trusting and because I taught him to be kind to everybody. So now I'm thinking it's all my fault. That if he had been a street-wise and shrewd boy then he would be alive today. But he thought the best of everyone and because of that he died, that's how it seems to me. I blame myself every hour of the day and I'll carry this guilt to my grave. The vicar has been to see me. I let him in because I don't want to hurt his feelings. He just stands there and he so desperately wants to help. He says that the only person who is to blame is the man who killed Jonas. He says I should remember Jonas with joy and cherish the memories, and I do because the memories are happy, but it's so hard. When I see other mothers with their children, I just want to scream. If I had another child, I would still have a reason to get up in the morning; now I'm just sitting there staring out of the window. My hands lie useless in my lap, no one needs me, no one bothers me. There's no point in going to bed at night, I don't need to get up in the morning. There is nothing to make me want to live the rest of my life.

'I used to sit by his bedside every evening. He would curl up under the duvet and his eyes would plead with me for comfort and encouragement, he needed so much support. We would talk about the day that had just passed and the day that was to come. I would think of some treat to look forward to, something to make him fall asleep with a smile on his face. That we would cook something special for tea the next day or watch a film together in the evening, the two of us, snuggled up on the sofa. All children deserve to have a treat every single day, all children deserve to be pampered.

'The worst moments are when my thoughts take control of me and I start to imagine what his last few hours must have been like. The pictures in my head are so disgusting they make me scream. What he had to go through. I don't know whether to think about it in all its horror so that I can suffer with Jonas or whether I should suppress it. The vicar says it's finished now and that Jonas isn't suffering any more, I'm the only one suffering now and he's right about that. I thought his funeral was so beautiful, the organ music and the flowers, and the poem that his teacher read out loud. I had to translate it into Norwegian for my parents, they don't speak any English. I visit his grave every single day. It took me for ever to choose his headstone; none of them was good enough. The one I chose was far too expensive. I had to take out a loan, but they were kind to me at the bank, they gave me a good rate. They all know about Jonas. The stone is heart-shaped with a cut-out in the middle and in it there is a lamp which lights up at night. There's an inscription underneath his name.

You were my darling angel.
Now there is only silence.

'Sometimes when I'm walking towards the church I notice how people stop at Jonas's grave. They stand there with a mixture of embarrassment and curiosity. It doesn't upset me, I like it that people stop and think, and then I wait until they've gone because I don't want to make them feel uncomfortable. I have reserved the plot next to him for myself, we're going to lie close to each other and I look forward to that. I'm not scared of dying. Jonas has done it, so I can do it too. I don't know much about eternity, but perhaps it's all right. I talk and talk and you listen with reverence. Perhaps you think that I'll be fine eventually because I can put words to my feelings. But the reality is that silence terrifies me.'

CHAPTER 40

'I've realised something,' Skarre said. 'We're always too late.'

'What do you mean?' Sejer said. 'Too late for what?'

'Once we arrive, the disaster is already a fact. Someone has lost control and the worst has happened. We can't ease the pain, either: isn't that a depressing thought?'

Sejer allowed himself a lenient smile. 'If you wanted to save lives, you should have become a fireman.'

Skarre circled the room restlessly. They were both waiting for the fax machine from which the result of Brein's saliva sample would soon emerge. They were paying the lab extra for a quick response.

'What are we going to do about Edwin?' Skarre asked. 'Even if we do get a perfect match, we have

197

nothing to link Brein to Edwin.'

'I know. It's going to be a long winter.'

'That reminds me,' Skarre said. 'I was in Kaffebrenneriet the other day with some friends. And in a corner was a guy I recognised.'

'Go on?'

'It was Ingemar Brenner.'

'Tulla Åsalid's boyfriend?'

'Tulla's boyfriend with a younger woman. At least twenty years younger. Blonde, attractive and giggling.'

'He must have finished with Tulla then,' Sejer said, 'and found himself a new girlfriend.'

'Or he's defrauding her,' Skarre said. 'Like he normally does. And I can't bear to think of that. Given what else has happened.'

'We mustn't jump to conclusions. Perhaps she's a relative. There's a lot we don't know.'

'Relatives don't snog each other,' Skarre said. 'I think we should warn Tulla, I think we owe her that. She's got enough to worry about as it is.'

'We're police officers,' Sejer objected. 'We don't get involved with people's love lives.'

'But this isn't about love,' Skarre argued. 'He's after her money.'

'I must remind you that Brenner has served his sentence. You have to give him a break.'

Skarre shook his head. 'Tulla's the one who deserves a break.'

'All right,' Sejer said. 'You win. Let's see if the right moment comes along.'

Skarre went over to the fax machine, bent down and stared at it.

'What are you doing?'

'I'm summoning up an answer,' Skarre said.

'Human beings are filled with psychic energies which we never use. I'm summoning them now.'

Sejer gave him a strange look. 'Now listen to me,' he said calmly. 'You don't like Wilfred Brein. You think he's a self-important and unsympathetic man and it would suit you very well if he turns out to be guilty. Elfrid Løwe would derive some small comfort and the general public would breathe a sigh of relief. But just because a man behaves brusquely towards the police doesn't mean he's guilty. Lots of people have very strong feelings about us.'

'Why are you suddenly lecturing me?'

'To save you disappointment,' Sejer said. 'The fact that he went up there doesn't link him to the crime. Besides, he does appear to have a bad hip.'

'Very well,' Skarre said. 'So he abducted Jonas August on one of his good days.'

He crossed the floor and opened the door to the corridor.

'Come on,' he said. 'Let's go down to the canteen.'

They found seats by the window and drank some Farris mineral water, faking a calm they did not possess. They waited. They watched people come and go. They studied the snowflakes falling outside. Muffled sounds drifted through the room, the clinking of glass and cutlery and muted voices. The smell of coffee. Skarre smoothed out a paper napkin. Sejer fiddled with his mobile phone, there were no new calls, no new messages. They waited. From time to time they glanced at each other across the table, then they looked away and sought out the window, the falling snow.

Finally they could no longer contain their

199

curiosity. They returned to the office and settled down in their chairs in deep thought. There was nothing more to say. It was during this loaded silence that the fax machine finally started whirring and the men shot up and rushed over to it. Sejer snatched the sheet, leaned against the wall, his eyes racing across the few lines. Then he let his hand drop.

'So what have we got?' Skarre asked.

'A match,' he said. 'Irrefutable, undeniable proof.'

CHAPTER 41

Brein opened the door. He was standing on his own two feet this time, but when they told him why they had come, he collapsed against the door frame.

'No!' he screamed. 'I want you to leave me alone!'

They allowed him a few minutes to sort out of a couple of essential things such as packing his blood-thinning medication, which he claimed his life depended on. He asked to call his father, but they told him no. He put a packet of cigarettes in his pocket and followed them to the police car. He did not utter a single word during the thirty-minute drive to the station. Sejer watched him in the mirror. Now it was Brein's turn to look like a small boy who had been abducted.

Once they reached the station he was placed in a cell, where he sat for four hours. He perched on the edge of the bench and stared down at his lap, at his hands with their blue veins. Several times he got up and went over to look out of the window. The cell faced a backyard with a brown Portakabin and several parked patrol cars. He saw Volvos and Fords. A row of green wheelie bins was lined up against the Portakabin. He paced the floor. He could take only a few steps before he had to turn around. He thought about those who had occupied the cell before him, thieves and robbers, murderers. He had nothing in common with them. He sat down on the bench once more and folded his hands. No one had come to check up on him, to see if he was all right, didn't they have to do that? They had promised him something to eat, but no food had arrived.

He felt a sudden urge to lie down and close his eyes, but it would be like surrendering, and he did not want to surrender, he was going to fight. So he continued to perch on the edge and to despair. He listened to the sounds outside, the traffic, scattered voices and shouts. Sometimes he would shudder violently, his heart racing; he had nodded off and woken up with a jerk. A cup of coffee would have been nice, he thought, another human being, a voice.

The four hours turned into a restless walk between the bench and the window; all the time he was trying to prepare himself for what lay ahead. Listen to me, he wanted to say, I can explain, it's not what you think! They seemed friendly enough and polite, and they did have rules to follow, but he didn't want to be naive, he didn't want to weaken, they weren't going to get him, they weren't going to pin something on him which wasn't true. For a moment he raged with

201

indignation at everything that had happened. He had been carried along by life itself, temptation had dropped right into his hands, and he had acted in accordance with his desires, it was like falling into a river and being swept along by the current. Wasn't he merely being human? He sensed how the heat surged through his body, and then he collapsed once more, because deep down he knew better, of course he did. They would show him no mercy, they would reel off their accusations, drag him through the mud like he was something inferior. Distraught, he tried to keep control of his thoughts, because it felt safer, but they overpowered him and he bowed his head in shame.

CHAPTER 42

Wilfred Arent Brein was not a handsome man. Nature had not been kind to him. He had a gaunt face and thin lips devoid of colour. He was conscious of his shortcomings and it showed; his eyes were evasive and changed, at times, to a sullen look.

'I was promised something to eat,' he began.

Sejer was reminded of a stray dog begging.

'Oh?' he said. 'Were you? We'll see to it. Presently.'

He sent Brein a questioning look. 'You haven't eaten much recently?'

Brein scowled at him. 'I think you owe me an explanation.' He tried to sound assertive, but there was not much strength left in his feeble voice.

Sejer leafed through a pile of papers on the

table, checked the time and read a few sentences on a document.

'Why haven't you been eating?'

'Surely it's my own business how much I eat,' Brein said. He jerked his head. It was a repetitive, nervous twitch.

'Of course,' Sejer said. 'I was just expressing concern. You've been having problems?'

'I live with a great deal of pain,' he said. 'I have done for years. Some days all I can do is lie on the sofa and groan. But you need to explain to me why I'm sitting here,' he added. 'You owe me that much.'

'I owe you nothing,' Sejer said, 'for the time being. If it turns out I've made a mistake, you'll get an apology. So far I haven't made a mistake.' Then, in a friendly voice, 'Did you know Jonas August?'

Brein jumped instantly. He had not meant to, he knew he had to be strong to save himself, but the boy's name rang like a bell in his ears and he shuddered. The room they were in was white, bare and windowless. The table, which separated them, had yellowed with age and the varnish had started to peel. There was something shabby about the furniture, as though it had been bought from some second-hand shop. On the ceiling a fluorescent tube cast a garish light over the stone floor. A camera had been placed in a corner of the ceiling. The lens followed him like an evil, foreboding eye. Sejer repeated his question.

'Did you know Jonas August?'

'I think you need to explain why I'm here,' Brein said again.

'You have no idea why you've been arrested?'

'No. I mean, come on. You can't just pick up people and put them in a cell like this,' he complained.

'Yes,' Sejer said, 'we can and I'm happy to get straight to the point. Let's not waste time; after all, you're hungry. This is about Jonas August Løwe. He was found on the fourth of September up at Linde Forest. The forensic pathologist has established that he was subjected to a violent attack, which caused his death, and we can link you to the crime with irrefutable evidence. Did you know him?'

Brein shook his head in disbelief. He was still unable to grasp the situation. Sejer's confidence frightened him, his composure and authority were menacing.

'Irrefutable evidence?' he stammered. 'No, I don't believe that.'

'DNA,' Sejer explained.

Brein rummaged around his memory feverishly, but he failed to see the connection.

'I haven't given you a sample,' he said. 'You're trying to entrap me.'

'You're already trapped. And if you're interested in telling your side of the story, then now is your chance. It's your best option. Jonas August didn't have that chance.'

Brein shook his head again. 'This is some sort of trick.'

'No,' Sejer said, 'it's very simple.' He changed tack. 'Did you know him?'

'I didn't kill those boys,' Brein said.

'I didn't say you had.'

'But that's what you're thinking. You think that I killed Jonas and Edwin, but I didn't!'

204

'We want to make sure we find out what really happened,' Sejer said. 'In order for us to do that, you need to work with us.'

'All right. But then you have to believe me, because I'm telling you the truth. I didn't know Jonas,' he said. 'I had only seen him a few times walking along the road, a little lad with skinny legs and trousers that were too big for him.'

He started digging a nail into a dent in the table. While he talked he avoided meeting Sejer's scrutinising eyes.

'I can't deny that I've been driving around looking at the kids,' he said, 'and pay attention to what I said. Looking at them, that's all. I know what you're thinking, but you're completely wrong.'

'You know nothing about what I think,' Sejer said. 'Go on.'

'I can't help that I'm attracted to children,' Brein said. 'I've always been like that. But I was too scared to tell anyone—you probably know this already. So I kept it all to myself, and that was very hard. It was a lot to handle for a small boy, because I was only ten when I started to have these feelings. There was a boy at the farm next to ours, and I was in love with him, he was only six, and I didn't know what to do with myself when he was around. I was all over the place.'

'So what did you do?' Sejer asked.

'I would watch him in secret,' he said. 'I would dream and fantasise. Needs must.'

'So you prefer boys?'

'Yes,' Brein said. 'Boys. I like their small bodies and their delicate limbs. I like that they are frightened and shy, I like everything about them, I

like the smell and the sound and the taste of them.'
He was growing more animated, his cheeks were gaining colour.

'How do they taste?' Sejer wanted to know. His face was deathly serious.

'Well, what can I say?' He shook his head. 'Like green apples.'

His words were followed by silence. The only noise was a low humming from the fluorescent tube on the ceiling.

'Can I smoke in here?' he asked hopefully.

'No.'

Sejer's reply was followed by another silence and Sejer waited. It would take time to uncover the truth, but he did not mind because he wanted to know. He wanted to map the crime down to the smallest detail. He wanted to measure and weigh it, turn and twist it, view it from every possible angle. His heart was beating calmly. He felt in control, in here he reigned supreme, in here he was, as Skarre put it, the man who could charm the birds off a tree.

'Were there any episodes you found particularly difficult when you were growing up?' he asked. 'It's quite all right to talk about such things.'

Brein gave him a despondent look. 'Everything was difficult,' he said. 'It was when I entered my teens that the trouble really started. Isn't it about time you got yourself a girlfriend, young man? You know what aunts and uncles are like.'

'I do.'

'So, of course, I was isolated,' Brein went on. 'I didn't fit in. I spent a lot of time on my own. Besides, I felt deeply ashamed about it all. People can't be serious when they tell us we need to come forward with our feelings, they've no idea how bad it is.'

'Yes,' Sejer said. 'I have an idea how bad it is.'

'I can only dream about what the rest of you take for granted,' Brein said.

'No one can take love for granted,' Sejer corrected him.

'No?'

'The world is full of people who watch the happiness of others from the sidelines.'

Brein rolled his eyes. 'Look around you,' he snorted. 'There are couples everywhere, walking down the street wrapped around each other; I can hardly bear to look at them.'

'Many walk alone,' Sejer countered. 'You're not the only one who is single. But perhaps you harbour an illusion that everyone else is granted everything their heart desires. It's not like that. What was your childhood like?'

'It was bad,' Brein said bitterly. 'And I don't mean to make excuses for myself, but it's only right that someone should know how bad it was. Perhaps you think my parents used to beat me, but they never raised a hand to me, it was far worse. There was coldness and hostility. My mum was always angry, it poured out of her in one constant, nagging stream. And she made so much noise, she slammed doors, she stomped around the house, her backside was the size of a rhinoceros. And she had a bizarre notion that you should always tell the truth, because she didn't want to be two-faced. So she always spoke her mind. It was the truth at all costs, in every situation. The truth in the shop, the truth across the fence to the neighbour, to door-to-door salesmen and to me. That I wasn't much to look at, that I wasn't all that bright. She scolded me and my dad. He would jump at the smallest chance to get out of the house. He would invent errands because he couldn't cope with her ranting. And they looked odd, the pair of them. Mum's build was coarse, loud and masculine, while dad was delicate and effeminate. It was like something was always brewing in the house, if you get my drift. And sometimes she would lock me out. I mean if I came home late, if she had told me a time and I had missed it, then I had to sit on the doorstep until she deigned to let me in. She would look at me, feign surprise and say, what are you doing out here? One winter, I actually froze to the top step. Another time I gave up thinking she would let me in at all, so I went down to the cellar. I spent the night there on some old sacks.' He let his hands flop helplessly. 'That was tough for a small boy.'

'Is she still alive?' Sejer asked.

'She got cancer,' he said. 'Her body was riddled with it, tumours everywhere. One of them was in the corner of her eye, it was pressing on her eye, it was disgusting. It looked like it might explode at any time. I didn't know where to look. You might say she was being punished for her neglect and betrayal, because she lay there for over a year, in great pain. I don't know how many hours I spent by her bedside, waiting. Listening to her breathing and hoping with all my heart that she would die. But she always pulled through and there would be more moaning and pain. I remember her last moments vividly. I was dozing on a chair. Suddenly she opened her eyes and screamed 'That's enough!' She twitched one last time and then she was gone.'

'How did you relieve your desire?' Sejer asked. 'I presume you found a way?'

He folded his hands on the table. His fingers were long and thin with sharp knuckles.

'I used pictures which I found in magazines, pictures of young boys. In PJs or swimming trunks. I made do with that. But once I was an adult I took a decision. I was adamant that I would have a proper life, like everyone else. I wanted to be like everyone else, it was crucial to me. I have some relatives up north, in Kirkenes. On a trip to see them I met a Russian lady. A lot of Russians cross the border for all sorts of reasons, but Irina had come to sell embroideries. Russian women really know how to sew.'

He glanced quickly up at Sejer as though looking for signs of contempt, but all he found was gravity and patience.

'We got talking,' he said, 'and I offered to buy her a cup of tea, and we talked for hours. Three months later we were married, and we had two daughters.'

'Are you still in touch with them?'

'No.'

'Have you tried to stay in touch?'

'Yes, of course, I have no one else. But I think Irina must have painted me in a bad light because they don't seem to be very interested. I wonder what she has told them. I haven't dared ask.'

'What are they called? How old are they?'

'Rita and Nadia, they're nineteen and twenty-two.'

'Do you miss them?'

Brein sighed. 'You know how it is. They don't

want to know someone like me. They're great girls, but it's best that I stay away.'

'Is that what you think? That you should hide away?'

'Yes,' he replied, 'that's what I think. And that's what you think, too. People would drive us into the sea, given the chance.'

Sejer looked at him calmly. 'There are clear reasons why you have developed this tendency,' he said, 'and it hasn't been established yet whether you need to be ashamed of it. A few things have been beyond your control; that applies to all of us. However, it could be argued, as far as the law is concerned, that you have a duty to take some precautions. And you didn't take them, did you?' Sejer looked at him closely. 'Jonas August is dead.'

Brein nodded. 'I just can't bear it,' he whispered.

'What happened to your marriage?' Sejer asked.

'It went down the drain, obviously,' he said. 'You know I had other needs. I felt I was playing a game, that I was false and miserable. And Irina felt neglected. So a distance was created between us and it grew over the years. I suppressed my real feelings until I was worn out. You don't know what it's like,' he groaned. 'It's exhausting.'

Sejer nodded.

'One morning she packed her suitcase and left,' he said, 'and I was all alone again. It was as if all ties were severed, I was cut adrift, I had nothing to hold on to. I was furious and angry and scared, I couldn't see straight. Other people don't have to worry,' he said. 'They're proud of how they feel, they think their feelings are good. That's what I think of mine. I would sit in my car and watch the kids from afar, while I daydreamed and fantasised.'

'You used to wait outside Solberg School, didn't you?'

'Yes. I liked the moment when the bell went and they poured out into the playground, like sweets out of a bag.'

'But you never touched them,' Sejer said. 'You only rolled down your window and talked to them?'

'I restrained myself,' Brein said. 'I'm forty-seven years old and I've always restrained myself. I just want you to know that.'

'You never invited them into your car?'

'I didn't dare,' he said. 'I couldn't trust myself completely. I would drive home and sit alone in my living room, alone with my longing. It's hard. It's like something inside is eating you up.'

'What was your job? Before you started receiving benefits?'

'I was a care assistant,' Brein said. 'I used to look after people. I really liked my job, I felt I mattered. But then the accident happened. I was knocked down on a crossing and injured. That was eight years ago. Since then I've spent a lot of time indoors. My only social life is the odd trip to the shops. And I watch telly all the time.'

'What was different about Jonas August?' Sejer asked. 'You finally made a choice; you invited him into your car. Tell me about it.'

Brein gripped the table.

'Yes,' he said. 'I'll tell you how it was. I'm fed up with all these rumours, that I'm a serial killer and worse, there are no limits to the stories in the papers. I drove around aimlessly. It wasn't the case that I had a plan, but I had a moment of weakness. I had passed Solberg Hill, I had just reached the

211

forest and it was very quiet. No people, no cars, just green fields of kale. There is little traffic on that stretch of the road. I passed a few farms and houses, but apart from that I felt all alone. By that I mean all alone in the world. Anyone who is different is also lonely. For ever. I drove quite slowly, and I thought how lovely the scenery was. Perhaps you don't think people like me notice those kinds of things, that we only have one thing on our minds, but that's not the case.'

'Don't underestimate me,' Sejer said.

Brein looked up with a sudden smile. His smile made his eyes shine. It softened his features, and in a flash Sejer saw that there was another side to Brein. A side which would seem appealing to a child.

'I spotted a small boy in red shorts,' he said. 'He was walking on the right hand side of the road and he was holding a stick. I was struck by the thought that the boy belonged to me, that providence had sent him and that I would finally be granted what I had longed for my whole life. I noticed how skinny he was, almost fragile, like spun sugar. We were at the bottom of the hill. When he heard the car, he stopped and stepped on to the verge while staring at me with his huge blue eyes. You know how kids stare at you, they ignore all boundaries. Do you know that feeling?'

'I do,' Sejer said.

' "You got far to go?" I asked him. He shook his head. "I live just up there," he said, "at the top of the hill, in the white house with the veranda." "Would you do me a favour?" I asked him, and yes, he would be happy to. I told him that the engine was playing up, that I had to look under the bonnet. Please would he get in and press the accelerator? He nodded enthusiastically. He threw the stick aside and got into the driver's seat. He struggled to reach the accelerator, but he was so proud of the job he had been entrusted with, and when he had revved the engine for a while and I had checked that everything was working all right, I offered to drive him home. Saves you having to walk up that hill, I tempted him. He thought about it for a while, as if he was weighing up the pros and cons. I could see how his mother's warnings were going through his head, but I flashed him my most brilliant smile and it made him drop his guard. He shifted over to the passenger side. And I was where I had always wanted to be: alone with a small boy. And it was overwhelming.' Brein paused. His gaze had reached the camera in the ceiling and his eyes filled with indignation.

'I asked him what his name was. Jonas August Løwe. A handsome name for a handsome boy, I said. That made him laugh a little, he was proud of his name, that was clear to see. I made him feel at ease and you may not believe me, but that's what I wanted to do.'

'I believe you,' Sejer said.

'Why don't we go for a ride? I suggested. Let's see what this old banger is good for. I pretended to be in a good mood. He agreed. He had no other plans and I could feel that he liked me, kids do, I'm good at talking to them, I make them feel they matter. I never experienced that feeling myself when I was a boy. Shortly afterwards we passed his house and he pointed out of the window. That's our house, he said, that's where I live with my mum. I raced brazenly past the house. It was him

213

and me, and nothing could stop me now. You should have seen him when we reached Granås, he was trailing me like a puppy.'

Brein looked up. He had talked himself warm and the nervous twitches had subsided.

'He spotted the wheelchair the moment we entered the living room. Yes, it used to be Mum's, you've probably guessed that by now, I haven't got round to returning it. He asked if he could have a go and I said yes. So he rolled up and down the living room while I watched him from the sofa. He had a great time with that chair. You can imagine how kids are fascinated by such things. I told him I could teach him to balance on two wheels, if he wanted me to. I was getting really excited, I don't mind admitting that, I had never been so close to a boy, but I was also getting desperate. I could tell where this was going and I was scared the people in the farmhouse might be able to see us, you know, the farmer who is my landlord, or his wife. Or his daughters, he's got four of them, or even the Poles in the barn. So I hardly dared breathe.'

Brein brushed his hair away from his forehead. There is something theatrical about the movement. He clearly wants to come across as a tortured soul and I suppose he is, Sejer thought, anyone who ends up in this room is a tortured soul, they're here because someone wronged them.

'I had some Coke in the fridge,' Brein said, 'and he wanted some of it. We sat next to each other on the sofa and chatted. He answered all my questions with a voice as clear as a bell, he was so modest, he was so obedient. His thighs were so thin and I could see his round knees, I remember thinking that they would fit my hand exactly. So I raised my hand and placed it carefully on his knee. And you may not appreciate this, but it was a very special moment for me.'

'How did he react?' Sejer asked.

'He sat upright like a burning candle. He looked down at my hand and I saw no alarm or anxiety, merely wonder. His skin was golden, covered by downy hairs. As I sat there, I was overcome by dread, that he would tear himself loose and run to the door. There was nothing in the world I dreaded more than losing what I had finally found. And though I didn't want to hurt him, I lost control. And my conscience did trouble me a little, but I brushed it aside. I thought it would all be over in a minute, after which I would take care of him and drive him home, you know, look after him in every possible way.

'I pushed him down on the sofa and pulled off his shorts. At that moment I heard something clatter on to the floor, but I couldn't work out what it was. And then I had my way with him. I just took what I wanted. When I came round, and it was all over, something happened.'

'What happened, Brein?'

Brein rubbed his eyes with his knuckles, and when he looked up, they were red and raw.

'He started wheezing,' he whispered. 'While I sat there looking at him, he turned blue.'

'And what did you do?'

'Nothing. I panicked.'

'Go on, Brein,' Sejer said.

'He started scrambling around the sofa,' Brein said, 'as though he was looking for something.'

'Jonas August was struggling to breathe,' Sejer said, 'and you sat

215

there watching him and you did nothing. How long before he lost consciousness?'

'Not long. I could hear something was wrong. And then he flung himself off the sofa and started fumbling around the floor, and I was upset because I didn't understand what was going on. Then he collapsed and lay still. I hid in a corner. I had no idea what to do.'

'What was he looking for, Brein? What was it that had fallen out of the pocket of his shorts?'

'An inhaler,' he whispered. 'I found it under the sofa.'

'Jonas August had asthma.'

'I know that now. But,' he put on a distraught face, 'it's too late.'

Sejer started walking around the room, all the time keeping his gaze pinned on Brein.

'Jonas August died in your presence,' he said. 'The one thing that could have saved him was lying under your sofa?'

'Yes.'

'You just sat there watching him struggling to breathe?'

'Yes.'

'You never once thought of calling someone or running out of the house to get help? This you have to explain to me.'

'I can't explain it. I felt cold all over. What will I be charged with?' he asked. 'Can you tell me that? It won't be murder, will it? Can you give me an idea of what my sentence will be?'

'Did it never occur to you that you had to save him?'

'You can't blame me for that.' Brein said. 'I had a panic attack.'

Sejer suddenly felt tired. He sat down in his chair again and closed his eyes.

'The charges aren't ready yet,' he said. 'You'll be told later.'

Brein gave him an expectant look. 'I was promised some food.'

'And you shall have some,' Sejer said. 'But don't ask me for sympathy,' he added. 'Talk to your defence lawyer. He's on his way.'

Now it was Brein's turn to get up from his chair. He positioned himself by the wall and his face was defiant.

'Perhaps you're the one who needs sympathy,' he said.

Sejer frowned.

'You're only halfway there and you know it. I never laid a finger on Edwin Åsalid.'

CHAPTER 43

Brein was transformed as if by a stroke of magic.

Gone was the bitterness, and the excuses, gone was the sullen look. He folded his arms and he straightened his back. He looked Sejer directly in the eye.

'I never laid a finger on Edwin Åsalid. I obviously know who he was; we can agree that he stood out, can't we? I used to see him walking along the road, poor lad, waddling along with all his excess weight, but we can stay here all night or till next spring for that matter, I'm not going to change my story. You've got to look elsewhere. He clearly got into someone's car, but it wasn't mine.'

* * *

'Brein is adamant,' Sejer said. 'And I'm inclined to believe him.'

'There must be two of them,' Skarre said. 'It is possible.'

'Or,' Sejer said, 'Brein is a first-rate actor. He confesses to one killing because he thinks it might be classed as an accident, hoping meanwhile that Edwin will never be found. And that consequently we'll never have a case against him.'

'Let's hope the prosecutor can find an expert witness who can prove that Brein's assault led directly to Jonas August's asthma attack and death,' Skarre said. 'Do you realise that the worst case scenario means he's convicted of manslaughter. He'll only get six years.'

'Yes,' Sejer said, 'but I don't concern myself with sentencing. And neither should you.'

'How many rounds are you going to go with him?'

'I don't know. I'm uncomfortable sitting in there with him. It feels like I'm wasting precious time and I can't afford to do that.'

He went over to the window and stared down at the traffic in the street. 'It's snowing,' he said despondently.

'A lot?' Skarre looked towards the inspector.

'Very heavily. I'm worried.'

'About what.'

'Time passing. We're bound to find Edwin sooner or later. But how much will be left of his body when we do?'

'I see your point,' Skarre said. 'We were handed

218

Brein on a plate. We won't be that lucky a second time.'

CHAPTER 44

Sejer went to see Tulla Åsalid and they talked for hours.

'Obesity is a big problem,' she said. 'Literally. The doctors frightened the life out of me. One of them once told me that fat people move so little that they don't develop muscles, and if they don't have any muscles, the blood can't reach the brain as it's supposed to. After that I lay awake all night. I think that might be what's happened. Perhaps his heart stopped and he's lying in a ditch somewhere.

'I never thought Edwin would become so big. He weighed five kilos when he was born and I was proud as a peacock because I thought it meant he was fit and healthy. But later he started gaining weight at a pace which terrified me. When he wants something, he looks at me with a power no mother can resist. It's a vicious circle, more food, more excess weight and more despair, which leads to him eating more, so he has some comfort at least. I think Edwin feels permanently ashamed of himself because he's so fat, and there is nothing I can do. He constantly helps himself to everything, he's unstoppable. It's all my fault. This would never have happened if Edwin had been slim and strong. I've cared for him for ten years and I'm responsible. I'm not strong. I can't bear to say no. When he looks at me with his brown eyes, I just melt.

219

'At night, in my dreams, I can hear him calling, but I can't answer him, I've lost my voice. He's trying to find his way home, he's stumbling in the silent darkness and I can't move, I can't see. When I wake up I'm overwhelmed by my powerlessness. Sometimes I want to run out into the forest and howl, pull up trees and bushes by the root and turn over rocks. He's got to be out there somewhere; after all, they found Jonas August in the forest. Ingemar once said that Edwin looks like a jam doughnut, large, pale and spongy. He wasn't being unkind, he was just joking and that's why I love him, and I can't expect him to behave like a father to Edwin, because he's not his father. They get on all right, I think, though I often wish that Ingemar would show a bit more interest. But I'm glad he's here now to support me, I wouldn't be able to cope with this on my own. Sometimes I console myself with the memories. All our trips to my cottage, Pris, which Edwin and I used to take. We would go for walks in the forest together and we would fantasise about outrageous meals, dinners, puddings and cakes and we would laugh so hard we would end up crying. I don't want to go there any more, I'm thinking about selling the place. Ingemar has promised to help me. He says I ought to invest the money, that he can take care of it for me and I'm grateful for that. I don't know anything about money and investments, or what will give a good return, so it's great that he'll deal with that.

'Something happened recently, which really upset me. I had a telephone call. And I didn't react with kindness, but with rage. It was Elfrid Løwe. She wanted to meet me. I couldn't help it, I lost my temper. She assumes that Edwin is dead, too, and that we have something to talk about, that we have things in common. I screamed at her, told her to stay away, and I slammed down the receiver. Afterwards I stood shaking like a leaf. I felt so upset. How could I have treated her like that? One day I'll have to contact her and apologise. But I do think she had some nerve, no one really knows what has happened to Edwin. Kids have gone missing before and they turn up and they are fine. I mustn't give up hope.

'Some children came to see me, it's a while back, now. Sindre was there, and Sverre and Isak and some of the girls from Edwin's class, I don't remember their names. They had made a kind of scrapbook with pictures and messages, the sheets were hole-punched and held together with red ribbon. 'We miss you Edwin, please come back,' things like that. Pictures of flowers and birds and animals, as children do. Alex Meyer had obviously told them to make this to show sympathy. I wasn't all that moved because I'm not sure how nice they actually were to him, normally.

'I'm still waiting for him, I wait every hour of the day, I wait as I lie in my bed, I wait as I cook, inside my head I hear my own voice crying out for Edwin. I'm convinced he'll be coming down the road soon with his rolling walk. I keep looking out of the window. I listen out for steps, or the door slamming. Whenever I hear a car pull up, my heart skips a beat. It might be the police or the vicar. I don't want the vicar to come round. I don't know what I'll do if he turns up. I used to go out a lot, now I mainly stay in. I can't bear to meet people. They look at me with compassion, but they avoid me because they don't know what to say. Imagine if they had dared to approach me! Hug me and comfort me. How are you? Is it bad? Is there anything I can do? But people are scared of feelings, that I might burst into tears, that they'll stand there not knowing what to do. I would rather have a grave than this uncertainty. The way things are now, there is nothing I can do for him. The feeling of powerlessness is overwhelming. It's all grief and despair and guilt, it's all emptiness and pain. What kind of life is this? I have Ingemar, of course, but he can't bring Edwin back to me. Still, he's the only one who can make me forget for a few brief seconds, the only one who can make me laugh. Afterwards I'm shocked that I could. It's as if I'm letting Edwin down in the worst way possible by being happy.'

CHAPTER 45

Sejer was often found hunched over the file, reading.

On the wall to the right of his desk hung a photo of Edwin as a constant reminder and sometimes Sejer would look up and ask him, 'What did you do, what happened to you?' He visited Alex Meyer. Meyer was happy to admit that Edwin had been a frequent visitor, sometimes with Sindre, or Sverre and Isak. Meyer had a steady gaze, as befits a man who has both confidence and a clear conscience. He talked about his class and everything they were going through. The children were having trouble sleeping. Parents had reported cases of bedwetting.

'We'll never know the full extent of this,' Meyer

said. 'The children are really struggling to cope.'

Sejer changed his approach and studied Ingemar Brenner's fraud convictions. Brenner was the only person in Edwin's circle with a criminal record. The man had a dubious talent as a con artist, but it was a big leap from financial crime to killing a child. Even if Edwin had been in his way. He asked Brenner to come to his office and he arrived at the agreed time. Sejer noticed his cream shirt and his shiny wine-coloured tie. Brenner was a man who went around relishing his own excellence. He was, in contrast to Brein, undeniably a good-looking man and he knew it. He was also brutally honest when it came to Edwin.

'I don't care much for kids,' he said. 'I don't mind telling you. They're unpredictable and I can't stand that.'

'You like being in control?' Sejer asked.

'I've never enjoyed being a spectator.'

'And whenever Edwin was in the room, that's exactly what you became?'

Brenner gave him a self-satisfied smile.

'I lecture,' he said. 'I'm used to an audience. I talk and people listen, you could hear a pin drop. And there's Tulla, of course, I've got her eating out of my hand.'

'Wouldn't you agree,' Sejer said, 'that your hands have got you into trouble before?'

Brenner stopped smiling.

'That's none of your business.'

'Perhaps not,' Sejer said, 'but we notice things and we draw conclusions.'

'You need to separate what has happened to Edwin from what my, formerly, generous girlfriends decided to give me,' he said. 'A woman

223

scorned will send you to the gallows, given half a chance.'

'The court didn't buy your version of events,' Sejer said, 'and neither do I. Tell me, what's your opinion of Edwin? What do you think happened to him?'

Brenner grew serious.

'It's obvious, isn't it?' he said. 'And excuse me for being so blunt. Of course, I haven't said this to Tulla, but like you, I think the following happened. Someone dragged Edwin into a car and drove him to the forest, where he was assaulted and later strangled. Or he had his head bashed in with a rock, what do I know? Afterwards he was dumped in a lake or maybe buried. It's a waste of time to speculate if he's still alive, I've no time for false hopes.'

'You don't like children, but are you fond of Edwin?'

'Let me put it this way, I'm used to him being there,' Brenner said. 'I'm used to him constantly eating, constantly begging. I'm used to the fact that he doesn't like me, that he thinks he has a monopoly on Tulla and that's wrong, of course. And it's their relationship that has turned him into what he is.'

'And what is he?'

'Well,' Brenner hesitated, 'a jam doughnut that keeps growing bigger and bigger.'

'Have you thought about moving in with Tulla?'

'I have.'

'Why haven't you done so?'

'I didn't want to become involved with Edwin's problems.'

'So you think of him as a problem?'

224

Brenner's hand checked and adjusted the knot in his tie.

'He's ten years old and he weighs nearly ninety kilos,' he said. 'Is there any other way of looking at it?'

*   *   *

A merciless winter hit the south-eastern parts of the country. The weather was relatively mild, but there were huge amounts of snow, wet and heavy snow that caused chaos on the roads, and people clearing their drives did their backs in. It snowed for weeks. When it finally stopped and the sky turned blue, the frost came and stayed for a month. People looked pessimistically at the gigantic snowdrifts. They will never melt, they thought, but then came April and suddenly it turned warm. People poured out of their houses lacking in everything: light, heat and fresh air. Tender dreams were formed. Perhaps life's worth living after all, they thought.

On one of these mild days Sejer drove up to visit Tulla Åsalid. He parked in her drive and noticed that the kitchen window was open, and as he got out of his car he heard a trickling laughter. He stopped to listen, confused, but then all he could hear was the wind playing with the treetops. How could she laugh like that? She had lost her most precious possession. Or was Ingemar her most precious possession; was she crazy, like her parents had said? He walked up to the house and rang the bell. It took a while before she opened. She started by apologising. She had been on the telephone.

Sejer explained why he had come.

225

'It's none of my business who you see,' he said cautiously, 'but when it comes to Brenner, then don't trust him with your money.'

She gave him a perplexed look. 'Why not?'

'Have you already done so?' he asked.

'No, of course not. Why would you say something like that?'

'Please don't ask me to go into detail,' he said. 'I don't like to expose people. I've come to give you some advice and I hope you'll take it.'

At this she looked haunted. She invited him in and they talked for half an hour. In the car on his way back he thought once more of her trickling laughter which he had heard through the window. Dear Lord, he thought, I can't blame her for having one moment of happiness. But still he could not shake it off, her laughter was like a sting and it troubled him.

*   *   *

Wilfred Arent Brein watched life go by from the window of his prison cell. He had settled in well. True, he fawned like a dog to the other prisoners, he kept his head down and he spoke in a low, mumbling voice. He was scared of their condemnation and waited on them like a servant. He lent them money and gave them cigarettes. This was how he managed to be left in peace and that was what he wanted. The day was divided into fixed routines. He liked the workshop and he liked the food. He liked helping out in the kitchen, all the smells and the heat from the cooker, the huge, steaming, bubbling pots.

He slept fairly well at night, curled up on his

bunk in a foetal position. He was serving ten years. On completing his sentence he would be released back into the community, back to his lonely existence on benefits, the same man with the same passion for young boys. He rarely thought about the day he would be released; life on the outside did not appeal to him. No one would welcome him, he would be left to his own devices, his own pain and his own urges. All things considered, prison life was not as bad as he had imagined. Every now and then a prison officer would stop by for a chat. Then he would come alive and talk himself warm about this and that, about his father whom he should have supported, the last book he had read, which had a sad ending. Society had already forgotten about him. New murders had been committed, new crimes that had been carefully planned, simple economic crimes for personal gain, which were obviously far worse that his own deed, which he had not wanted to commit anyway. He was driven by his passions. He was adamant when it came to this. It was the notion that saved him, which meant that he could sleep at night. He slept a dreamless sleep.

*   *   *

However, spring had finally arrived now, lush and teeming with life. Teenagers bloomed like the crocuses in the flowerbeds, they unfolded and started flirting with each other, they hung around on street corners, they lay on the grass in parks. The snow on the fields of Fagre Vest Farm finally melted, and the mound with its few bushes became visible; it lay like a small island in the fields and pretty rowan trees grew on it. Early one April evening a group of young people walked down towards Loch Bonna. One of them was Signe Lund, who worked behind the till at Kiwi. She had swapped the green uniform for a red miniskirt; her round knees were milky-white after the long winter. There was her cousin, Mai-Britt, small and chubby, with a mass of ginger hair, puffing away at a Benson & Hedges. Ellemann and Rolf were at the front, determining their direction, and Signe sensed what it was all leading up to.

Inside the mound in the field was an earth cellar, and last summer she had lost her virginity there. She was consumed by trepidation twinned with fear of what she wanted and yet at the same time did not want, but life was like that, and boys always got what they wanted anyway and she did not want to come across as uptight. Neither did Mai-Britt. They meandered across the fields and punched each other playfully. They were so full of life and they were up for anything. Walking in the wet soil was hard work and they were worried that they might be spotted by the farmer from Fagre Vest who would set his Alsatian on them. After all, they were trespassing.

They sat down on a large stone. The boys circled the girls like sheepdogs herding sheep, but something distracted them and interfered with their chat. A smell. A dense, rotten vapour drifted through the air. The older of the boys, Ellemann, got up to investigate.

'It's coming from the earth cellar,' he said.

Excited and nervous he started looking for the trap door. He stamped the ground methodically with his heavy boots. Soon they heard the sound of heels against wood. They cleared away some grass and leaves, and none of them said a word because the smell was unnerving and it frightened them.

The trap door was bolted.

Its rusty iron hinges groaned and whined as they opened it.

CHAPTER 46

Edwin Åsalid lay on an old sprung mattress.

He lay on his stomach with his arms outstretched and he looked like a beached whale. There was a fair amount of rubbish inside the earth cellar, magazines and old newspapers, wrappers from chocolate bars, and empty beer cans. A rotting wooden ladder with four steps led to the bottom and the ceiling was low. A long time ago the earth cellar had been used for storing potatoes. Years later the town's children had discovered it and put it to new use. Thanks to the frost the body had kept well and it had been protected from damp and animals, but now the mild weather had set in, and it was starting to decay.

There was a crowd of onlookers on the road to the loch. The police vans also had to park there. The crime scene officers had to carry their equipment across the fields.

Skarre snapped off a long piece of grass.

'What do you think?' he asked.

'Not a great deal so far,' Sejer said.

'He's dressed. He's not naked from the waist down like Jonas was. Perhaps we should be grateful for that.'

'Perhaps.'

Skarre started chewing the piece of grass.

'The killer is from Huseby,' he said. 'He has to be, he knew about the earth cellar.'

'What's the name of the farmer?' Sejer asked, nodding towards Fagre Vest.

'Skagen. Waldemar Skagen.'

'Was he questioned when Edwin went missing?'

'Yes.'

'We need to interview him again.'

'Will there still be evidence of sexual assault after such a long period of time?' Skarre wondered.

'I hope so,' Sejer said. 'Snorrason won't miss a thing.'

'How big is the earth cellar?'

'Six square metres? Or what do you think? The local teenagers have clearly been having a good time on the old mattress. Perhaps there is nothing else to do down there in the dark.'

'Will they finish this evening?'

Sejer looked at the men working away.

'I hope so. I want Edwin's autopsy carried out tomorrow morning. I hope Snorrason finds something. What do you think of the hiding place for the body?'

'Clever, obviously,' Skarre said. 'No one would come here in the winter, and he didn't have to dig a grave. All he had to do was shut the trap door and bolt it.'

'And if the local youth hadn't been in the mood for love this very evening, Edwin could easily have lain there the whole summer,' Sejer said.

A crime scene officer walked past them with a

bag. Its contents were visible through the clear plastic.

'This is what we found,' he said. 'Do you want to take a look?'

Sejer took the bag.

'Remove the topsoil,' he said, 'and sift it. Check every twig and blade of grass. Let's hope he's left something behind. Have you found any weapons yet?'

'No.'

Sejer held up the bag and studied its contents. 'One copy of *Hello!* magazine,' he said, 'and one of *VG* magazine. A packet of Petterøe cigarettes, empty. Cigarette stubs with and without filters. Two cans of Frydenlund beer, bottle tops. A comb missing practically all its teeth. Candle stumps, orange peel. A hair band. That is a hair band, isn't it?'

'Yes,' Skarre replied.

Sejer continued looking at the contents of the bag.

'Do you recall what the boys were doing down on the jetty the day Edwin went missing?' he asked.

'They chatted about Alex Meyer,' Skarre said, 'and they ate sweets.'

'Correct,' Sejer said. 'Jelly turtles.'

He pointed at the bag. 'And here's the empty packet.'

231

Snorrason was an unhurried and methodical man with a mild and gentle view of the world, and he was moved by the body of the child who lay before him. A few parts of Edwin's body were covered by light grey corpse wax, a heavy, swollen substance which replaces fatty tissue. It was this wax which had preserved his body during the last eight months. Now his chest had been opened up and the ribs removed. His internal organs had been weighed, examined and placed in steel basins on the autopsy table. His liver, kidneys and his heart which had beaten for ten years. The smell was raw and acrid, a blend of something sweet and cloying, and something else, reminiscent of fish entrails. The strawberry-blond forensic pathologist got hold of an oscillating saw to open up his cranium. Its whirring sound screeched through the autopsy room, and an odd, burning smell filled the air.

'A ten-year-old boy weighing this much will have experienced numerous problems,' he explained. 'Knee pain, sores, aching joints, shortness of breath. At worst, diabetes. As far as his mental health is concerned, the pressure would have been huge. He wouldn't have been able to keep up with his friends, his life must have been a major struggle with a great deal of stress. In addition, I'm sorry to have to conclude that if his weight gain had continued, he would never have lived to see old age. Sooner or later his heart would have given out from the strain.'

For a while he worked in silence, then he

continued to ponder the curse of obesity.

'Moreover,' he went on, 'obese people decompose faster than thin people.'

'Why?' asked Skarre.

'Because of the amount of subcutaneous fat. Fat insulates and prevents heat loss and heat causes the body to decompose. Do you follow?'

Sejer nodded. He measured one metre ninety-six and he weighed eighty-three kilos. It followed that he could expect to decompose at an average rate, but he was unsure whether or not this should be regarded as an advantage. He watched the pathologist secretively. He wondered how his job affected him, if it made him think of his own mortality, the decomposition of his own body or his children's.

'Have you found any evidence of abuse or strangulation?' Sejer asked.

Snorrason shook his head.

'Nothing at all,' he replied, 'not so far. No external signs of violence. His larynx is intact. No fractures to his skull, no signs of lesions or stab wounds. Blood and tissue samples have been sent to Toxicology, it will be a week or two before I'll get the results. But as I said, so far, nothing.' He looked up. 'Are you surprised?'

'No.'

'He died as a result of dehydration.'

'You're telling me he died from thirst?'

'Lean forward and let me show you something.'

Snorrason lifted Edwin's right hand up from the steel table.

'Look at his fingers, look at his nails, they're torn to shreds.'

'He was trying to claw his way out through the

trap door,' Sejer said.

'I'm afraid we'll have to assume so.'

'This means he was buried alive,' Skarre said. 'What kind of death is that?'

'One of the very worst,' Snorrason said. 'It takes a long time to die from thirst. In Edwin's case, I would imagine that it took him a week. Four to five days at least. He would have lain all alone in the darkness growing weaker and weaker. He would start to feel nauseous. The nerve cells in his brain would start to malfunction, his heart would be unable to beat at full capacity, his blood would start to thicken in his veins. He would have been in a profound state of distress and been delirious. He would have cried out for his mother and he may have been praying to God. Finally he would have fallen into a coma.'

'And this,' Sejer said, 'is what we have to tell Tulla Åsalid.'

CHAPTER 48

They left the building.

They inhaled the fresh air deeply.

They crossed the car park and got into the car. Frank Robert, who had been waiting on the back seat, poked his nose between the front seats to beg for a treat. Sejer gave him a dog biscuit. Skarre rolled down the window. Life had become so visible after death in the autopsy room. The cloud formations in the sky, the swaying treetops, the sun reflected in a window, parked cars. Two nurses walked across the car park in front of the hospital.

Skarre followed them with his eyes; their white uniforms were practically luminous in the spring sunshine.

'He found nothing,' Skarre said.

'No,' Sejer said, 'but that in itself is significant.'

'I've got a theory, but I refuse to believe it.'

'So do I, but it's all we've got. Who would trap another person?'

'Kids,' Skarre said.

'Precisely.'

'I can see the initial attraction. But surely they would have let him out. After a while. After a few hours.'

'Well, would they?'

'Of course. They can't trap one of their friends in an earth cellar and then go home to bed.'

'They may have trouble sleeping,' Sejer said.

The two men looked at each other, then they both shook their heads. Sejer took out his mobile and found a number.

'What are you doing?'

'I'm calling Alex Meyer.'

After a brief conversation he put the mobile back in his packet.

'Sverre is having trouble sleeping,' he said, 'and Isak has started wetting the bed.'

CHAPTER 49

Mathilde Nohr positioned herself by the window.

Her silhouette was sharply defined against the light outside. She placed her hands on Sverre's shoulders, a demonstration of ownership, and

235

there was a smile on her lips, but it failed to reach her eyes. She had asked Sejer to give her a reason for the meeting and his reply had scared the living daylights out of her.

Isak and his father had sat down. His father was as thin as a rake, his hair and eyes were dark. It seemed as though everything was hard for him: his son, this meeting, life itself. Isak was silent and pale, his brown freckles clearly visible, scattered across his cheeks like a fine spray of mud. Sejer looked at the two boys. He noticed that Sverre's right hand was in plaster.

'What happened to your hand?' he asked.

Sverre looked away. 'I broke my finger.'

'Broke your finger? How did you do that?'

No reply.

'We've found Edwin,' Sejer said. He looked at Sverre. 'Do you know where we found him, Sverre?'

'In the earth cellar at Fagre Vest Farm . . .'

'Did you hear that on the news?'

Sverre traced circles on the floor with his foot. 'Mum told me, she heard it in the shop.'

'What about you, Isak?' Sejer said. 'Did you know where we found him?'

Isak was twining his fingers so fiercely that he, too, was in danger of breaking them.

'Have you ever gone down there to play?'

'Not often,' Sverre said reluctantly.

'But you have been there? The two of you together?'

Sverre shrugged. The parents were on their guard as if they knew deep down that at any second, life would turn around and bite them.

'Someone trapped Edwin in that earth cellar,'

Sejer said, 'and for some reason no one came back to let him out. We don't understand why.'

'Pardon me for asking, but what are you insinuating?' asked Mathilde Nohr. She had bags under her eyes. She had lain awake all night staring into the dark.

'I'm hoping I've found an answer,' Sejer said. 'There is not a single scratch on Edwin's body, no one has beaten him or abused him, or hurt him in any other way. Someone trapped him in the earth cellar and we think it might have happened as part of a game. He was with Sverre and Isak on the tenth of September, that's why I'm asking them what happened. If perhaps something went wrong.'

Sverre threw a glance at Isak, but Isak kept studying his hands.

'You need to tell us what happened,' Sejer said, 'and no matter what it is, you will not be punished, no one will hit you or send you to prison.'

At this Isak's father stirred. 'Edwin was picked up by someone in a car,' he said. 'Are you calling my son a liar?'

'I'm not accusing anyone of anything,' Sejer said. 'I'm trying to get the boys to explain themselves. They both have mobiles. Both are in their parents' names, and when we checked them out, we discovered that they called each other several times on the night of the tenth of September. We have a list of five calls in total, the last one made around midnight.'

He looked gravely at Sverre. 'That was when you called Isak and you spoke for three minutes. What was so important that you had to talk to him in the middle of the night?'

'We didn't do anything, really,' Sverre

237

whispered. He emitted a small yelp like a puppy that has got its paw caught in a door.

'I'm sure there is an explanation,' Sejer said, 'and I need it. I need it now,' he added, 'because this business with Edwin has been going on for so long and we are all exhausted.'

Suddenly Sverre started talking. 'We were just sitting there,' he said, 'on the mattress. Just chatting. The trap door was open so we could see what we were doing. We watched Edwin eat the sweets.'

The boy's voice was frail and small. Again he looked at Isak, but received no help from him.

'What were you talking about?'

'Football. Carew. And Solskjær. That's all.'

'Go on.'

'We were starting to get bored.'

'How long were you there?'

'Dunno. I didn't look at my watch, but I decided to climb back up and Isak followed me. We stood at the top looking down at Edwin, he had trouble getting up the ladder because he was so fat and some of the steps were broken. He had two steps to go, but then he slipped and fell down and he kept doing that. We rolled around laughing because it looked so funny.'

'So you didn't help him?'

'We tried pulling him up, but he was too heavy.'

'Then what did you do?'

'We gave up. We shut the trap door.'

'Why?'

'Dunno. We just did. We pretended that he was our prisoner. It was really cool.'

'And you bolted the trap door?'

'Yeah, we bolted it. And Isak jumped up and

238

down on top of it, but it was just for fun.'

'Were you paying him back for something?'

Sverre adopted a guilt-laden expression. 'He told on us.'

'Whom did he tell?'

'Everyone. Meyer and all the other teachers. He was such a tell-tale.'

'You had been stealing sweets from the shop, hadn't you?'

'Only sometimes.'

'What did Edwin do when you bolted the trap door?' Sejer asked. 'Did he call out for you?'

'No, it was all quiet. He just sat there. We thought he would start screaming.'

'And then,' Sejer said, 'you went home. Why did you do that?'

'It was tea time,' Sverre said, 'and we thought he could sit there until we had finished eating.'

'Just for fun?'

'Yes, just for fun. Just for a little while. He would be all right on the mattress.'

'I see,' Sejer said. 'So this is what happened: you left Edwin in the earth cellar and went home. You had your dinner. What had you and Isak planned afterwards?'

'That we would meet up outside the Kiwi shop. That we would walk back together and let him out.'

'So why didn't you?'

'I wasn't allowed,' he said.

'What?'

'Mum wouldn't let me go back out.'

Mathilde Nohr gasped.

'It was Gran's birthday,' Sverre said.

Sejer looked up. 'It was your gran's birthday and

239

you were supposed to visit her?'

'We were going over to her house with her present. I did know it was her birthday, but I had forgotten all about it. I said I was going out with Isak, that we had to do something really important, but Mum said no. She said that Gran was more important. Then we started arguing. And then Dad joined in and he got really angry and we all ended up screaming at each other.'

'And you were afraid to tell the truth? That Edwin was trapped?'

'Yes.'

'What would have happened if you had told them the truth?'

Sverre looked at his mother again. 'I've got to do what my dad tells me,' he whispered.

'I understand. But what happens if you disagree with your dad?'

Sverre looked at the floor.

'Don't you want to answer?'

'No.'

Sejer kept looking at him. 'Is it supposed to be a secret?'

'Yes.'

'Did you talk to Isak?'

'I called him. I told him he had to go there alone, but he didn't want to. It was late when we came back from Gran's. I had to go straight to bed.'

'Did you plan to let him out the next morning?'

'Yes.'

'You told us Edwin got into a car,' Sejer said. 'Why did you do that?'

'I had to tell you something. So I thought it would work if I told you someone had picked him up.'

'Didn't you think of the consequences?'

'We thought it would be all right.'

'In what way would it be all right?'

'I don't know. But if we told the truth, we would be in really big trouble.'

Sejer got up and wandered around. The sight of the two boys made him feel infinitely sad.

'Yes,' he sighed, 'there will be really big trouble.'

CHAPTER 50

The public judged the adults and the children.

There had always been something about Sverre and Isak. They were known to shoplift, and there was something about their parents, too; they had clearly failed. The public required an explanation and they thought they had found it.

Kristine Ris had discovered something, too, and she was delirious with happiness. She stood in front of the bedroom mirror and studied her body, she was motivated by something new, something strange. A sense of pride and a strength she had no idea she possessed filled her head and her body and she decided to take action. She tore the wardrobe doors open. On the top shelf was a brown suitcase. She pulled it out and placed it on the bed and started packing. I'm leaving now, she thought quickly, while he's out. That way I'll avoid all the accusations, I'll leave now while I feel strong. I'll be fine, I'm better off without him. All these years he has kept me down, now I'm going to start a new life where he can't tell me what to do.

Yes, I've used him, but I feel no guilt. He'll blame me for everything, but I'll tell it like it is, that I can't live in this house any longer. At the back of her mind she was aware that he might try to cause trouble for her, but if he did, she would just have to deal with it. She had rights too, and she would be able to get help and advice. She packed underwear and socks, jumpers, trousers and tops, a dressing gown, a nightgown, some toiletries. Things she would need for the first few days. She went back to the living room, to the desk, where she picked up the telephone and called a cab. She waited by the window and she felt the warmth of the sun. She was going out into the light.

She left a note on the coffee table.

I'm leaving, I want to live my own life.

She imagined him reading the few words. His jaw would clench in defiance, a curse would echo between the walls.

The cab arrived, she got in and soon they were off. She closed her eyes, let it all sink in, her sudden freedom and everything that would happen. It took half an hour to drive to the motel. It consisted of eight tiny separate yellow huts each containing two single beds, a sink and a mirror. Next to the huts were a petrol station and a café where she could get something to eat. She collected the key from reception and let herself into the small room, put her suitcase on the floor and lay down on the bed. Carefully she placed her hand on her stomach: it was growing in there and it would start kicking by summer. It would all become known one day and Reinhardt would be furious. The fear of what might happen rippled through her. My child, she thought, my baby.

Muted laughter emerged from the hut next to hers.

CHAPTER 51

'What are you thinking?' Sejer asked.

'I was remembering my father's anger,' Skarre said. 'It was terrifying. There was nothing I feared more than that. He was an authoritarian and a very old-fashioned man, and I was brought up to fear and love him. Whenever he got angry, it was like he underwent a transformation, he grew one size bigger, literally. He would open his mouth and start a scolding which would blow the curls off my head, then he would turn his back on me and storm upstairs. I would hear the sound of his footsteps and a door slamming. After a while he would stop walking up and down and he would descend to announce my punishment, which would be grounding me for a week or two, or stopping my pocket money.'

'Sverre's father beats him,' Sejer said.

'I know,' Skarre said. 'What can we do about it?'

'I've given him my telephone number. Perhaps he'll call.'

'There's not much evil in him,' Skarre said. 'Just fear.' He looked at the inspector. 'There is something I've been meaning to ask you. Do you remember Andor? The chap we met down on Guttestranda?'

'Of course I remember Andor.'

'Did you move your chair?'

'Yes, I did.'

'And? Is your psoriasis better?'

'Now that you mention it, it is, actually. But apart from that he was totally on the wrong track with those visions of his.'

'Not at all,' Skarre said. 'And it's strange, I hardly know what to say. We found Edwin in the earth cellar lying on a mattress. I went on the net and looked up "Hasselbäck" and yes, it's a place in Sweden, in Västmanland. But I also discovered that Hasselbäck is the name of a sprung mattress from IKEA.'

*   *   *

Sejer drove up to Linde Forest and parked by the barrier. Elfrid Løwe was sitting next to him, her hands resting in her lap.

'This is where he parked the car,' Sejer said. 'He carried Jonas the rest of the way.'

She looked at the barrier.

'This is where he met the couple who later identified him. Without them we would never have caught him. Shall we get out?'

She opened the door and put her feet on the ground. Sejer walked around the car and took her arm. She felt the warmth from the setting sun and the strength from the man next to her.

'Brein is a pathetic creature,' she said.

Sejer nodded. 'I'm sure you're right. He has settled into life in prison, he says his days are fine. I ask him if he thinks of Jonas, if he repents. He says every single hour of the day.'

'Do you believe him?'

'No.'

They walked on in silence. Sejer tried to match

244

his long stride to her short steps.

'Did you take a lot of photos?' she asked.

'Yes, we did. We have to, they're an important part of the investigation.'

'What happens to them when the case is closed?'

'They're filed with the rest of the documents. No outsider will have access to them, if that's what you meant. If I were you, I wouldn't ask to see them.'

'I haven't.' Then in a milder voice. 'The weather was fine, wasn't it? Do you remember how warm it was last September, summer temperatures.'

'Yes.'

Sejer recalled it. 'We were working in shirt-sleeves. The day after, it grew cooler and the autumn set in.'

They were further into the woods. Sejer held some branches back and Elfrid ducked under them.

'He chose this place with care,' Sejer said. 'People are complex. Despite the awful thing he had done, he tried to do something right. Jonas should not be found in a ditch.'

'You don't expect me to be grateful for that, do you?'

'No,' he smiled. 'I was just thinking out loud.'

Finally he saw the clearing. He recognised the small cluster of trees and the log pile.

'Here, Elfrid, by those trees,' he said.

She stopped. Put her hand over her mouth.

'He lay face down,' Sejer said, 'with his arms by his side.'

'And without his trousers,' she said.

'Yes. That was how it was.'

'What did you think?' she asked. 'What was your

first thought when you saw Jonas lying there without his trousers?'

'I wondered what I would say when I met you. I was also relieved. He was whole and fine.'

She smiled a brave smile.

'It's a fine place,' she said. 'Very fine.' She sat down on the logs. Sejer remained standing looking at the scenery, all the smells of the forest wafted through the air.

'His punishment was far too lenient,' she said.

'Brein's, you mean?'

'Yes.'

'What kind of punishment do you think he deserved? What would have satisfied you and Jonas?'

'Not the death penalty,' she said quickly. 'You didn't think that's what I meant?'

'Not for one second.'

'Well,' she hesitated. 'I don't want him to have too much nourishment. And I don't mean food. I mean all other sources of nourishment, for the soul and the heart. Experiences, warmth and kindness.'

'He'll have some of those. Does that torment you?'

'Yes. His days shouldn't be good.'

She looked up at him with despair in her eyes.

'Imagine if he's laughing right this moment,' she said. 'Sometimes I can see him laughing. It's unbearable.'

'But he'll have his dark moments, too,' Sejer said. 'Alone in his cell. And he has nowhere to go.'

'There are many like Brein,' said Elfrid.

'Yes,' he said. 'As long as adults make mistakes and as long as parents abuse, they will create new abusers.'

246

'Thank you,' she said softly.

'What are you thanking me for?'

'Everything.'

'Please forgive me for putting it this way,' Sejer said, 'but it has been a privilege to know both you and Jonas August. I wouldn't have missed it for anything.'

They walked back to the car. They did not speak for a long time, but finally when they reached the main road, she turned to him and asked:

'Can I call you?'

'Of course.'

'I mean, can I call you when things get really bad?'

'You can call me any time,' he said. 'We know each other now.'

'There's a bond between us,' she said, 'and I need to keep that bond for ever.'

*   *   *

That night it started to rain.

Yet he stayed in the park, there was nothing for him to go home to, the rooms were empty and cold. She had left him in the most cowardly way imaginable and she had planned it carefully. He felt a violent need to vent his rage, but he gritted his teeth. He was not going to whine, it was not his style. There was a grid of narrow tarmac paths in the park. He wandered around aimlessly. Soon he reached a crossroads. In the centre of it was a rotunda with a pretty statue of a little girl, she was naked. He slumped on to a bench and watched her. She was frozen mid leap, she was laughing and her arms were outstretched. He started thinking she was coming towards him, that at any second now she would jump on to his lap, but when he tried to catch her eye, she stared blindly past him. The rain trickled down the back of his neck and his shoes were letting in water, but he stayed where he was. Things would turn out the way he wanted them to, sooner or later. A little girl would emerge from the trees, she would be wearing a red raincoat, and he would get up from the bench and flash her a dazzling smile.